KIDNAPPING THE PRESIDENT
WASN'T GOING TO BE EASY

The tent-flap rustled and President Arthur stepped out. He looked tousle-haired and sleepy, his pale legs barely showing under a dark robe he had belted around his middle. Slocum froze where he was, scarcely breathing, watching the Commander-in-Chief urinate.

When Arthur bent to duck back into the tent, Slocum made his move . . .

OTHER BOOKS BY JAKE LOGAN

JAKE LOGAN

THE JACKSON HOLE TROUBLE

BERKLEY BOOKS, NEW YORK

This is a work of fiction and does not claim to represent historical truth. However, several of the characters are based on actual personages, and many of the incidents (such as those involving Nick Wilson, Lieutenant Doane, and Chief Washakie of the Shoshone) did happen as recounted herein.

THE JACKSON HOLE TROUBLE

A Berkley Book / published by arrangement with
the author

PRINTING HISTORY
Berkley edition / March 1983

ISBN: 0-425-06139-6

A BERKLEY BOOK ® TM 757,375
Berkley Books are published by Berkley Publishing Corporation,
200 Madison Avenue, New York, N.Y. 10016.
The name ''Berkley'' and the stylized ''B'' with design are trademarks
belonging to Berkley Publishing Corporation.

PRINTED IN THE UNITED STATES OF AMERICA

1

Slocum woke to the faint sounds of somebody trying to get into the stable.

For a long moment he lay quietly in his bedroll, unable to see in the dark, not sure that he'd really heard anything. He held his breath and listened.

The sounds had stopped. His bay stirred uneasily in its stall against the far wall, then subsided. All Slocum could hear now was the distant clop-clop of a horse moving at a trot on some street closer to the center of town. The hoofbeats grew fainter and faded into the distance, leaving only dead quiet. Then the sounds came again: hands fumbling at the long wooden bar laid across the stable entry.

Slocum pushed his blankets down. The straw crackled beneath him as he rolled to face the big double doors.

Thin slivers of moonlight slanted down through the cracks in the walls and the place smelled of stale hay. The stable was abandoned and dilapidated. The loft had collapsed, and most of the stalls had been busted up for lumber, but the doors were still sound. Slocum had forced a stick through a crack in one of the doors and into a knothole in the wooden bar outside to keep it from sliding open, but the stick wouldn't hold long against that persistent fumbling at the door.

He figured it had to be four in the morning. He had bedded down shortly after two. Broke and unable to afford a hotel even in a town like Green River, he had considered himself lucky to find this empty stable. It was possible that the man outside had the same problem and the same idea, but it didn't pay to take chances.

He eased himself up out of the bedroll and began slipping his pants on.

Half-dressed, he thrust his Colt down into his waistband and felt around in the hay until he found the old singletree he'd kicked against when he'd laid his bedroll down. The singletree, about three feet long and capped with metal at both ends, would make a good weapon. The bay was all he had left that was worth anything, and he didn't want to risk shooting his own horse in the dark.

Gripping the singletree in one hand, Slocum crept back through the hay into the dark on the side opposite the row of stalls. He crouched down out of the moonlight slanting through the walls.

The man at the door had located the stick Slocum had thrust through the hole in the sliding bar. Slocum could hear him working at it now, trying to nudge it back out of the hole. The sounds were slow and cautious. If this was just another saddle tramp looking for a place to bed down, he was being awful quiet about it.

He heard the final rattle of the stick being pushed through the hole and the small thump as it dropped to the floor inside. Carefully, quietly, the wooden bar was slid back off the doors. One door creaked slowly open, and the man slipped inside.

Slocum held himself very still. The man had halted

just inside the door, as if to let his eyes adjust to the deeper darkness within. He was only a vague form in the moonlight coming through the door behind him, but Slocum could see the gun in his hand.

Not somebody looking for a place to spend the night, then. But Slocum had no idea why else anybody would be sneaking in here; from the outside, it seemed obvious the stable was abandoned and empty. And, so far as he knew, he had no enemies in Green River.

He had arrived in town barely four hours before, around midnight, looking to meet up with Clay Bellows, who had agreed to take him into his market-hunting operation, supplying game to the army and the Indian agencies. But Bellows wasn't due in till morning, and Bellows was the only one who even knew Slocum was on his way to Green River.

The bay shifted and stirred in its stall across the way. Slocum saw the man dip through a slice of moonlight and move in that direction. Maybe a horse thief, then. The man could have seen Slocum enter the stable earlier and then waited till he was sure to be asleep. And the bay was a good horse, worth a hundred dollars, at least.

He watched the man fade into the darkness of the stall. The bay shied and jerked at its halter rope. Slocum heard vague shushing noises and the sounds of the man's hands patting the horse's flanks. He hefted the singletree, listening. If the man started leading the horse out, he would have to stop him in here; outside, on foot, he would never catch him. He was just bracing himself for a rush when he heard a creak at the door and another man eased inside.

Two of them. And they weren't after the bay. The first man had come back out of the stall, passing through a patch of moonlight, and was moving cautiously to the right, toward where Slocum had left his bedroll. Slocum watched him go down on his knees, feeling around the saddle laid there for a headrest. The second man was still at the door. He had a gun out, too, and Slocum could see him scanning the dark overhead, likely looking for the loft.

The first man turned back toward the door and called out in a hoarse whisper, "He ain't here."

The second man swore and ducked into the dark of the row of stalls. His boots struck a board and he swore again. Then there was silence. The silence stretched through a long minute. Slocum didn't move.

Finally the first man called out in that same hoarse whisper, "He ain't here, I tell you."

The second man didn't answer, most likely waiting to see if this careless talk was going to bring trouble out of the dark. Finally he said, "Your luck he's not, giving us away like that. If he was, you'd be dead by now."

"Maybe he went out," the first one said. "To a saloon or someplace."

The second man started creeping through the dark toward the bedroll. "What about the loft? Maybe he heard you coming in. Maybe he's in the loft."

"There ain't no loft. I know this place. The loft's collapsed. All that hay there's where it came down. His horse is stalled and here's his bedroll, but he must have gone out."

"We saw him come in. If he went out, we should have seen him."

The second man had reached the first. Now he too went down on his knees and started searching around the bedroll. Suddenly he came up into a crouch. "You fool! A man don't go out without his boots. He's in here somewhere."

A sudden scramble sent them both out of sight, back into the dark toward the row of stalls again. Slocum tightened his grip on the singletree, eyes straining to see where they'd gone. He couldn't figure what they were after. If they knew anything about him at all, they must know he was dead broke; otherwise, he wouldn't be sleeping in this stable. It had been a while since he'd done anything to bring the law on him; if they were after him for something like that, it would have to be on a pretty old warrant. Besides, they didn't act like lawmen.

The side walls on most of the stalls were gone, but the pillars were still standing. Likely that was where they were hiding. And they wouldn't stay there forever. He knew men in situations like this. The waiting was worse than the risk. Sooner or later, one of them would move.

The bay shifted and stirred, its hindquarters banging up against the side wall. He heard what sounded like a muffled whisper to the right of that, but he couldn't make out exactly where. Then one of them moved. He saw the vague shape of the man against a crack of light in the far wall, and he whipped the singletree around and hurled it as hard as he could through the dark.

He hit the floor as soon as the singletree had left his hand, but even so he heard the impact: the dull thunk of a metal-tipped end against the man's skull and the clatter as the weapon ricocheted to the floor. The man dropped like a stone.

"Ed?"

It was the voice of the man who had entered the stable first: one quick, scared word, followed immediately by silence, as if the man had suddenly realized he was giving his position away. Slocum waited, his Colt out now and pointing through the dark, watching the area where the voice had come from. He could hear the breathing of the other man, quick and heavy, frightened now, knowing Slocum was somewhere here in the dark and that he himself was alone, his partner down and maybe dead. From the sound of his breathing, the man wasn't moving. Probably sheltered behind one of the stall pillars, keeping it between himself and where he figured Slocum was.

"Slocum?" The hoarse whisper came from across the stable.

Surprised, Slocum shifted the Colt in the direction of the voice. He didn't answer.

"Slocum? Don't nobody mean you no harm, Slocum. There's somebody wants to talk to you. The man sent us to get you."

A strange way to send for a man you wanted to talk to. Slocum figured it for a bluff, a way to get him to answer, to let the other man know where his position was. The silence seemed to swell like air in a balloon. He was pleased to hear the other man's breathing continue loud and scared. A frightened man meant an easier opponent. But it was clear the man wasn't going to move. Slocum was going to have to bring this to a head himself.

Carefully, he rose to his knees again, counting on

the hay behind him to keep from being silhouetted against the light. He got his feet under him in a crouch, braced himself, and came up in a rush, leaping to the right.

He landed in more hay and rolled, trying for the shelter of a pile of lumber from the ruined loft. A gun flashed near the far wall, and he heard the frantic scramble of the man running for the door before he'd even stopped rolling.

By the time Slocum got himself righted and turned around, the other man was already through the door. Boot steps sounded on the street outside, running south. Slocum leaped to his feet and flung himself out the door.

The man was already forty yards ahead, running along the deserted back street, staying in the shadows of the building fronts. Though the moon was bright, Slocum couldn't see a horse anywhere, only the dark shape of a buggy at the far end of the street. His quarry seemed to be aiming for that, but Slocum was gaining. He had closed to within twenty yards when somebody swung out of the buggy and seized the fleeing man by the shirtfront.

The two were struggling when Slocum reached them. He was surprised to see that the man from the buggy wore the blue of an army uniform with the shoulder straps of a colonel.

"That's him," the other man spluttered. "Damn it, Colonel, let me go. You got your man. Let me go."

The colonel made no move to release him. Tall and broad-shouldered, with a look of authority at least equal to his rank, he gave Slocum a quick once-over. "You're John Slocum?"

"Yes. You mind telling me what this is all about?"

The colonel ignored him and turned back to the other man. "Where's your partner?"

"Still in there. Slocum hit him with something. For all I know, he's dead."

"I doubt he's dead," Slocum said. "I brained him with a singletree." He still had his Colt out, and now he pointed it at the colonel like an accusing finger. "Maybe I ought to brain you, too. You still haven't told me what this is about."

The colonel's eyes met Slocum's but he didn't seem to take the threat very seriously. He placed his free hand on the barrel of Slocum's Colt, as if to see whether it had been fired. Then he released his hold on the other man's shirtfront and pushed him away. "I told you no shooting."

"I got a right to defend myself. Your man here didn't know you wanted him alive. He might've killed me."

The colonel nodded toward the stable. "Go get your friend. Drag him out of there if you have to. Then get out of Green River. You've been paid. I don't want to see you again."

When the other man was gone, the colonel removed a long black cigar from an inside pocket and stuck it between his teeth. He watched Slocum over the flare of the match, a faint smile at the corners of his mouth. "You did a good job. Better than I expected, considering it was two to one. I expected to see you brought out here unconscious."

"I take it this was your idea," Slocum said. "I don't feel real friendly toward a man that sets his dogs on me. Maybe you'd better do some explaining."

"I wanted to find out if you were as good as you were said to be. You can put that pistol away. Come to my hotel at noon tomorrow and we'll talk.'' He tucked a scrap of folded paper into Slocum's pants pocket. ''This'll tell you all you need to know for now. Come see me tomorrow. If we agree on things, there'll be more of those. Five hundred more, to be exact.''

The colonel swung back up into the buggy seat and flicked the reins, and the buggy started away along the street. Slocum saw that the other man had dragged his partner out of the stable and was helping him away. The one he had brained with the single-tree was upright but barely conscious; he had an arm draped around the other's neck and was weaving and stumbling along the edge of the street, still in a daze. When the two of them rounded the far corner, Slocum stuck the Colt in his waistband and removed the scrap of paper the colonel had tucked into his pants pocket.

On it was a name, a street address, a hotel name, and a room number . . . and folded inside was a greenback bill. He unfolded the greenback and held it up in the moonlight, where he could see the numbers at the corners of it.

It was a hundred-dollar bill. Five hundred more of those, the colonel had said. Fifty thousand dollars, to be exact.

2

By eleven-thirty the next morning, Green River was as crowded as a fairground on the Fourth of July.

From the time he'd left the stable after shaving and washing up in a trough out back, Slocum had found himself in a steady stream of wagons and buckboards and buggies and riders. All of them were headed in the same direction he was and all the people were in a fine high state of excitement. The narrow boardwalks were crowded with family groups, young mothers carrying babes in arms, drifters, drunks, cowhands, shopkeepers, and what looked to be a whole school full of youngsters in the care of a prim young teacher. Slocum kept the bay to the center of the street, unable to make out what all the excitement was about or to understand the cause of it. He had never seen a town like Green River so crowded this early on a weekday.

Everybody seemed to be headed toward the train station square. The hotel where the colonel was staying was located there, so Slocum let the crowd's current carry the bay along while he thought about the man he was going to meet. Colonel Smith, it said on the paper. A little obvious for an alias, maybe, but Slocum had no doubt that it was one. A man didn't track another man down, as the colonel had obviously tracked Slocum down, and offer him a job worth fifty thousand dollars, unless what he had in mind was on the far side of the law. And that was the part Slocum found was bothering him.

He was thirty-nine years old, and he had had too many years of riding the high line. That had been fine in the first few years after the War, with the South gone down and Slocum himself driven west by Reconstruction, stripped of everything he'd ever had or believed in. But that kind of life began to wear on a man after a certain age. And that was why he'd come here hoping Clay Bellows would take him on as a market hunter. It was something he'd done before and could do again, and it wasn't a bad way to make a living: out in the open, dependent on nothing but his skill with a gun, with nobody to answer to but himself and maybe a partner or two. He still had nothing to believe in. After thirty-nine years, all he had was a horse and what time was left to him. Lately he'd begun to realize that that time was all he was ever going to have, and that perhaps he'd better find a way of life that wouldn't have him spending what was left of it in some territorial prison.

So the colonel's offer wasn't exactly what he was looking for right now, but it would bear investigation. Fifty thousand dollars was a lot of money.

The crowd was beginning to bunch up in front of him, slowing to a halt. He saw a line of blue-uniformed troopers blocking off the street up ahead, and now an entire cavalry troop passed behind that thin blue line, every man in his parade best and sitting erect in the saddle, boots and brass polished to a high shine, the right-guide up front carrying a guide-on flag fluttering in the breeze. The troop trotted on past, the clatter of hooves rising up above even the hum of the crowd, and when it had passed on, the foot soldiers broke up the line and the crowd surged forward again. Slocum nudged the bay ahead, wondering what the cavalry was doing there. There was no troop posted to Green River that he knew about. The nearest forts were Laramie, where he had just come from, and Washakie, up in the Wind River reservation.

The crowd surged out into the train station square, thinning out some with more ground to cover. Slocum worked the bay left along the row of buildings fronting the near end of the station platform and dismounted. The crowd was going no farther; it eddied up around the station platform like a river dividing around an island, joining a throng already gathered there. The station itself was draped with colorful bunting and American flags, with streamers hanging from the rooftops. Whatever this was about, it had all the flavor of a patriotic holiday. And he didn't know of any patriotic holidays in August.

The hotel wasn't the kind of place he would have expected a colonel to select for his lodgings. Like most hotels near train stations, it wasn't first class and it didn't look to get the best run of customers. The clerk in the dim little lobby directed him up a creaking flight of stairs. He found the room number he was looking for and rapped twice.

The colonel opened the door himself, freshly shaved and in a newly pressed uniform. "Right on time," he said. "Come on in. Let me offer you some coffee."

The suite wasn't much, but it was probably the best the hotel had to offer. They were in a sitting room, with a window looking out onto the station square and a couch facing two stuffed chairs across a small table. On the table was a tray bearing a pewter coffee pot, mugs of cream and sugar, and two cups.

"It's good coffee," the colonel said. "The one thing that's good in this hotel."

"All right, I'll have some, then."

"Fine. Fine."

The colonel bent to pour coffee into both cups, his uniform coat tightening across his back as he did so. He had a broad back, to go with the broad shoulders, but his waist and hips were slim, and Slocum could tell that the uniform was very well tailored. The colonel was a big man, bigger than Slocum, with a broad mouth that could wear a smile to make a man feel important and hard, sharp eyes that would tell a smart man not to believe the smile. He cut an impressive figure.

He finished pouring the coffee and handed Slocum a cup, that diplomatic smile on his face. "I'll let you decide on the cream and sugar. Help yourself." Then he picked up his own cup and went to lean against the windowsill and look down on the crowd in the square.

Slocum took his coffee black and joined the colonel at the window. The crowd had grown larger since he'd entered the hotel. More people were surging in from the street he had come down, and the square was so full that buggies and wagons had come to a complete stop, like little islands marooned in a sea of milling people. He was looking directly out toward the near end of the platform, and now he saw that only two sides of it were full. The area on the left was roped off to keep the crowd back, though he could see a couple of carriages parked along that side as well. The tracks stretched away to the east of town. There was no train in sight.

"Quite a reception," Slocum said. "Must be somebody pretty important due in on that train today."

The colonel cut a sharp glance at him. "You don't know who they're waiting for?"

"I just got into town last night. Which reminds me—how did you know where I was?"

"I set those men to look for you. They tracked you all the way from Fort Laramie after they finally found you. Your coming here was a fortunate coincidence. Now I can show you what I'm after."

"Which would be what?"

"Sit down, Mr. Slocum." The colonel waved to one of the chairs and took a seat on the couch facing it. "Let's talk about you." He lit one of his long black cigars and picked up a sheet of paper from the table between them. He read aloud: "John Slocum. Age thirty-nine. Born and raised in Calhoun County, Georgia. Fought for the South in the War of the Rebellion and rose rapidly to the rank of major. Fought at Vicksburg, Antietam, and Chancellorsville, among others." He glanced up at Slocum. "You had a good war record. It says here you were reduced to captain for striking a subordinate—a lieutenant, I believe—but that you continued to serve well until the surrender."

Slocum shrugged. "That lieutenant panicked and ran under fire. If I hadn't stopped him, he'd have had half the troops running after him. But that's all old history. You wouldn't maybe tell me where you got it?"

"From Confederate army records. They're still on file in Washington."

Whoever this colonel was, he seemed to be important, with access to files all the way back in Washington. "You obviously want some job done," Slocum said. "Something worth fifty thousand dollars, if I understand you correctly. You don't mean me to believe you went digging through old Rebel army files to find a man to do it for you."

The colonel smiled. "No. I found my man first. Then I went looking for what I could learn about him." He picked up a second sheet of paper and quickly scanned its contents. "From all the evidence, went West immediately after the War, like a lot of men mustered out of the Rebel army. Drove cattle out of Texas, worked as a cowhand, a teamster, a market hunter. Drifts from pillar to post, living by his wits. Has a reputation for being a gunman. Wanted in several territories on charges ranging from stage holdups to bank robbery." The colonel glanced up at him, as if to check his reaction. "Wanted in at least one on a charge of murder."

"Not guilty," Slocum said. "I may have worked more than one side of the law in my time, but that don't make me unique out here. And that was a while ago. I make my living the best way I can, but I try to do it legal. And I've never murdered any man. Killed a few, maybe, but only when they were trying to kill me." He nodded toward the sheet of paper the colonel had in his hand. "You didn't get that from any Rebel army file."

"No. I didn't. When it became apparent to me what I was hunting for, I went to the one man who could tell me where to look. Allan Pinkerton. You've surely heard of Pinkerton. His agents have been on your trail more than once. And some of these charges against you are still outstanding.''

The colonel was looking at him, the eyes curious, watchful, a smile just faintly visible at the corners of that broad mouth. Slocum recognized the statement for the threat it likely was; the colonel wanted Slocum to know that he had a hold over him—that whatever it was he wanted him for, it wouldn't be wise for Slocum to reject it.

From outside the window came the high, thin scream of a distant train whistle. The murmur of the crowd welled up from below. The colonel rose from the couch and waved Slocum to the window. "Let's take a look. I want you to see this."

The train was still a dark line in the distance, heading directly toward them. The crowd had surged up around the platform, a line of blue-uniformed troopers holding them back. The rooftops around the square were lined with onlookers, and on the roof of one building Slocum saw a man with what looked to be a device for making photographs, a big box-like thing on a stand with a black cloth draped over it.

The crowd's buzz seemed to grow louder; here and there he saw a man holding a youngster up on his shoulders so the child could see. From beyond the far side of the platform came a bugle call, and now he saw the troop of cavalry he'd passed in the street come wheeling into the roped-off area to the left of the station, files passing in and out of files, turning and cutting and fancy-dancing into perfect parade formation. The bugle sounded again and they reined to a halt facing the station.

"Troop G, Fifth Cavalry," the colonel said. "Seventy-five good men and true." He seemed to be taking a great deal of pleasure in the sight—a military man pleased to see a display of military precision.

"I take it this train has something to do with whatever it is you're offering the fifty thousand for," Slocum said.

"Not the train, but what's on it." The colonel retrieved a small black valise from a corner of the room and laid it open on the couch. "That's not your ordinary passenger train out there."

The train was coming into the station, slowing now, a tall arch of black smoke trailing back over the cars. A band had struck up a march from somewhere beyond the cavalry troop. The men lining the rooftops around the square were already waving their hats, and the one with the photograph machine had his head stuck under the black cloth draped over it. Then the engine disappeared under the roof of the station platform, and the train shuddered to a halt in a loud hiss of steam.

The colonel had been putting together a long spyglass he had taken from the valise. Now he brought it to the window and set it on a folding stand in front of Slocum. "Here. Look through this. I want you to get a close look at some of the people on that train."

Slocum pulled up a chair and dipped his eye to the lens of the spyglass. For a moment he saw nothing but a blur, then he worked the focus around till the end of the platform came sharply in view. He edged the stand to the left till he saw the cavalry troop and the carriages parked along that side. A group of what looked to be local dignitaries was climbing from the carriages onto the platform, accompanied by an army officer. He followed them with the glass until the left edge of the train came in focus. Now a pair of troopers swung out of the first car and stood on either side of the door. They were followed by a short, erect man in a blue uniform, wearing the campaign hat of an officer.

"You recognize him?" the colonel said. "General Philip Sheridan. Commanding general of most of the districts west of the Mississippi. You ought to remember Sheridan. He gave you Rebs a lot of trouble during the War, in the Shenandoah Valley, particularly. They say he's slated to become commander of the entire army before the year's out."

Slocum watched the general going along the row of local dignitaries, shaking hands. Short, stocky, and long-armed, he looked like a peppery little rooster, very pleased with himself. The sight of him left a bad taste in Slocum's mouth. He had a strong memory of the valley of the Shenandoah and the devastation Sheridan's troops had left behind. More men, most of them civilians, were filing out of the train now. The first one, a white-haired gent, had started along the row and was shaking hands.

"That's George Vest," the colonel said. "Senator from Missouri. There's Colonel Sheridan, the general's nephew. Behind him is Robert Lincoln, son of the Great Emancipator. He's Secretary of War now. Doesn't look like his father, does he? Doesn't have his father's force, either. There. There's the man we're waiting for. The one shaking hands now. I want you to take a real good look at him."

Slocum centered the spyglass on the portly man in suit and vest going along the row shaking hands. He could tell by the response of the little group of dignitaries that this one was even more important than the men who had preceded him. From the swell of noise below, the crowd knew it, too.

"That," the colonel said, "is the President of the United States."

Surprised, Slocum brought the spyglass into sharper focus. The man looked to be in his fifties, with a drooping moustache and muttonchop whiskers which extended down along his chin. Despite having just debarked from what must have been a long train ride, he looked elegantly turned out. His clothes were expensive, and a bright gold watch chain was looped across his vest.

"What's his name?" Slocum asked.

When there was no answer, he raised his head to find the colonel staring at him. The band was still pumping out that march down below.

"What's his name?" the colonel said. "I told you, he's the President."

Slocum repeated it. "What's his name?"

The colonel regarded him with some consternation, as if not sure he was serious. "President Arthur," he said. "Chester A. Arthur."

Slocum brought his eye back to the lens of the spyglass. The portly man had finished shaking hands and turned now to wave at the crowd. Head on like this, Slocum could see that he was tired, could see the effort it cost him to hold that smile while he waved. Somebody had taken him by the arm and was pulling him back toward the edge of the platform. He turned and was swallowed up in the group of army officers and dignitaries moving toward the carriages ranked along the side of the station. When the entire party was aboard the carriages another bugle sounded and the cavalry troop broke formation, one squad riding on ahead, others flanking the sides of the carriages as they pulled away from the platform. A final squad fell in at the rear, and then the crowd broke through the line to surge after them.

Slocum watched until the little cavalcade had disappeared around a corner at the far end of the square. Then he raised his head to find the colonel watching him, those hard, sharp eyes scanning his face.

"What's the President of the United States doing in Wyoming Territory?" Slocum asked.

The colonel drew slowly on his long black cigar. "He's on a vacation."

"He's come two thousand miles for a vacation? In this country?"

"That's right."

The colonel was still studying his face, as if expecting to read something important there. Now he moved the spyglass away from the window and sat down on the couch across from Slocum. He leaned back, drawing on his cigar, and there was something keen and bright in those hard eyes. He seemed at ease but alert in a way that Slocum had begun to see was natural to him. The man was full of some restrained energy that came off him like a scent and seemed to make those broad shoulders strain against the confines of his uniform.

"This was decided back in May," the colonel said, "after the President dedicated the Brooklyn Bridge in New York. Notice was taken then that he seemed unusually fatigued, and the press began speculating about his health. So it was arranged that he come out here on a pack trip, camping and fishing. He and his whole party will be going into the back country

for a month. Presumably up into Yellowstone—
Senator Vest is a sponsor of the park there—but the
exact route isn't known.''

''And what do I have to do with all this?''

''One thing I want you to know,'' the colonel
said. ''I am not acting as an individual in this. I
represent the United States government. Some might
not see it that way, but I do and those I represent
do. You've exiled yourself out here, Mr. Slocum.
It's fair to guess you have no interest in the U.S.
government or in what goes on back in the States. I
do, and it's enough that you believe what I tell you.

''The state of affairs of the country is not good.
The government is in a mess. I will not go into all of
it, because it's not necessary that you know about it.
But it might interest you to learn that Arthur fronts a
faction of the Republican Party that is anti-South.
They call themselves Stalwarts as a sign of their
loyalty to the cause of keeping the South down. As
you probably know, the South is suffering from the
effects of the war and Reconstruction to this day.
The other faction of the party is known as the
Halfbreeds, because their loyalty to that cause is in
question.''

The colonel took a sip of his coffee, his forceful
eyes watching Slocum over the rim of the cup as if
to see how all this was affecting him. Slocum recognized the appeal to his Southern loyalty, and he
didn't like it. It was a little too obvious. He had no
way of knowing if anything he was hearing was true,
but he was beginning to be very impressed with the
colonel. The officer sat without moving anything but
the hand that held his coffee cup and his cigar,
totally at ease. His easy grace would fit well into

political salons and social gatherings. This was a man who would make general some day, and a high-ranking general at that. For the first time it occurred to him that the man just might be a general, passing in the guise of a colonel. There were a lot of colonels, even out here, but a general was a rarer thing.

"I will tell you how much of a mess the government is in, Mr. Slocum," the colonel said. "Chester Arthur is not even an elected President. The man last elected President was James Garfield. Garfield was part of the party faction known as the Halfbreeds, and he ran on a ticket with Arthur as his vice-president, in an attempt to unite the party, the government, and the country. The attempt failed. Four months after he became president, Garfield was assassinated by a member of the Stalwart faction, a man who admitted his aim was to elevate Arthur, the Stalwart, to the White House. And now Arthur is out here, going into the wilderness for a month."

"I'm waiting to hear where I come into this story," Slocum said.

The colonel nodded, almost as if in approval. "You have a good record as a leader of men," he said. "Both during the War and in your various exploits out here. You have the reputation of a man who can organize an operation, who is not afraid to use force if he has to, and who is good at it when he does. That's what I want you for, Mr. Slocum. Because there are those of us who have the firm conviction, even if we cannot yet prove it, that Chester Arthur became President of this country by conspiring in the assassination of his predecessor, James Garfield. And we believe it is our duty to the government and to the country to see that this is brought to light."

The colonel leaned forward now, his hard eyes on Slocum's face. "Arthur and his party will be going up into the back country, far from prying eyes. All newspaper reporters have been barred from the trip. He will be cut off for the entire month. What we want, Mr. Slocum, is for you to organize a force that can get into that camping expedition and take Arthur out of it. We want you to abduct the man, at some point previously arranged, and turn him over to us."

3

It was three in the afternoon by the time Slocum found his way to the Wolf's Den Saloon, where he was supposed to meet Clay Bellows.

The town had thinned out some, but not a lot. When he halted the bay at a cross street to let a pair of buggies pass, he saw a crowd gathered up the street, likely in front of the hotel where the Arthur party was lodged. Several of the passersby were carrying small American flags hawked by some merchant enterprising enough to see profit in the occasion, and a few of the drifters along the boardwalks had already had too much to drink in honor of it. By nightfall, when the family groups had withdrawn to their homes, Green River would likely go on a spree.

It made him feel a little uncomfortable, riding through this crowd with two thousand dollars in his pockets—the advance payment from the man who was calling himself Colonel Smith. Almost as uncomfortable as accepting the money had made him. He wasn't sure he wanted any part of the colonel's plan. Right now he planned to talk it over with Bellows and see if he could get it clear in his own mind. If he decided to go ahead with it, Bellows would be a good man to have along.

The Wolf's Den was a dingy one-room saloon

owned by an old friend of Bellows's, a former trapper and scout named Jim Fisher, who had taken up barkeeping when his age had forced him into a less strenuous life. Fisher was sitting on a high stool behind the simple bar at the back of the room. Several loungers in front of him were getting an early start on the night's drinking. The few tables scattered about were empty, and the loudest sound was the buzzing of flies circling over spilled liquor on the bar-top.

Slocum crossed to the corner of the bar and caught the old man's eye. "You seen Bellows?"

Fisher nodded. "He was looking for you. Got in here about two hours after midnight last night. You're not going to find him happy. Started drinking as soon as he got here and didn't stop till he passed out. Drinking on credit. He's dead broke."

Slocum was surprised. Bellows should have just completed filling a contract for the Wind River reservation up at Fort Washakie. The major portion of the payment came on fulfillment of the contract, and even Bellows couldn't have drunk up that much money between here and Wind River.

"You know where he went?"

"Didn't go anywhere. Couldn't move." Fisher jerked his head toward a door around the corner of the bar. "I put him up back there. You'll likely have to wake him, and you can bet he's got a hell of a headache."

Slocum peeled a bill off the roll in his pocket. "You'd better let me have a pint of that stuff, then."

He went back through the narrow hallway to the dirty little storeroom where Fisher had put Bellows up. The room was almost empty. The afternoon light filtered through the one smudged window in the wall. A stack of crates stood in one corner. Bellows was flung out on his back on a pallet in another corner, still in his clothes, his floppy hat just covering his eyes. Slocum squatted on his hams at the foot of the pallet and uncorked the pint bottle.

Sprawled in sleep as he was, his mouth open, Bellows showed every year of his age, which was somewhere over fifty. His beard was streaked with gray and his greasy hair hung to his shoulders. He'd been one of the last of the mountain men, a trapper, fur hunter and squaw man, and he still wore the trappings of his trade: thick moccasins, fringed leggings up to the knee, long buckskin jacket beaded and fringed in Indian fashion. An oversized Smith & Wesson .44 was strapped up high around his waist, a Bowie knife in a sheath on the other side. He had aged a lot since Slocum had known him, especially in the past three years, after the army had cut him loose, his services as a scout no longer needed now that most of the Indians had been pacified. That had been the last job Bellows had taken any pride in. He had recruited his Crow scouts himself, training them and working with them until they could match any Indian unit in the army. Something had gone out of him when they had been disbanded and returned to the reservation, and in unguarded moments like this, it showed in his face.

Slocum reached out and shook him by one moccasined foot. "Clay? Wake up. It's Slocum."

Bellows grunted and stirred, his hat falling down away from his eyes. He flinched in his sleep and jerked away from the light coming through the window.

Slocum shook him again. "Wake up, Clay. It's three in the afternoon."

Bellows's face scrunched up as if to ward off sound, and a small twitching set in around his eyes. He rocked his head back and forth, popped one eye open to see who was shaking him, then closed the eye again.

"I hear you tied one on," Slocum said.

Bellows felt around on the pallet for his hat. His dry tongue came out and licked his lips. "You got anything wet on you?"

"Here." Slocum held out the pint. "I figured you'd be needing this."

Eyes still closed, Bellows fumbled in the air until he found the bottle. He brought it to his mouth without even raising his head and took a long pull. He rolled the whiskey around in his mouth and swallowed it. "Glad you got here," he said. "Wasn't sure I was going to make it." He set the hand holding the bottle down gently beside him, his eyes clenched tight. "You mind closing them curtains?"

Slocum got up and dragged the dingy curtains across the window. When he turned back, Bellows was hauling himself upright and propping himself against the wall. He still hadn't opened his eyes.

He took another long pull on the bottle. "Fisher tell you what happened?"

"Told me you got in here dead broke last night. Said you drank yourself into a stupor and passed out back here. Didn't tell me anything else."

"Didn't tell you why. I got myself swindled. Spent three months hunting game, trusting my partners, and when the time came to get paid off, they cheated me out of my share. Left me flat busted. It was all I could do to get here.''

''I got here broke myself. Just last night.''

''We're a lucky pair, ain't we? I was glad you weren't here when I got in last night. With no money to outfit us and me promising we'd go in together on the next contract, I didn't want to see you. Might not even have come down here, but I was tracking those back-stabbing partners of mine, and Green River's where they ended up. Couldn't find them last night, but that's the first thing I intend doing today.''

''Maybe we ought to talk first. I've run onto something here in Green River we might be interested in. Something likely dangerous, but worth talking about.''

''All there is here in Green River is my money, and I aim to get it back.''

Slocum heard footsteps approaching along the hallway and turned to see Jim Fisher come in with a bucket of water and two bar towels. Fisher set the bucket down beside Bellows and tossed a bar of soap onto the pallet. ''I been asking around a little for you, Clay. Your friends have signed on to an expedition the army's putting together. That business I told you about last night. They're culling mules out north of town.'' He draped the towels across Bellows's knee and started back toward the door. ''You'll find them in those corrals out there if that's still what you're aiming at.''

When Fisher had gone out, Bellows handed the bottle to Slocum. ''Here, hold this,'' he said, and stuck his head down into the bucket of water. He came up dripping, his long hair streaming down his face, and went to mopping himself up with one of the towels. "How fit are you feeling?" he asked. "I aim to go kick me some ass. I'd welcome some help, but it ain't really your affair, so I'll understand if you butt out. But we can't outfit ourselves till I get my money back."

"Could be we don't need that money," Slocum said. "I got plenty right now. If we decide this other thing's worth going into, we could maybe make enough to put working for a living behind us."

Bellows was still rubbing his hair dry with the towel. He cocked one eye at Slocum, eyebrows raised. "Sounds dangerous, all right. And worth talking about. But not till I take care of this other little business. Right now I don't want nothing else on my mind. And, like I said, I'll understand if you don't want no part of it."

"Well, Clay, we'll be working together no matter what. So I figure your trouble is my trouble. Couldn't let you go two-on-one, anyway."

"Good. I appreciate it." Bellows ignored the bar of soap. He recorked the pint bottle, stuck it into his pocket, and hoisted himself to his feet. "Let's go find ourselves some trouble."

4

The army was selecting mules for its pack train in a large lot behind a sprawling stable about a quarter of a mile north of town. There looked to be over two hundred mules milling around in a series of corrals and holding pens stretching back behind the stable, and a couple dozen mule skinners and troopers moving among them. Slocum and Bellows reined off across a weed-choked ditch about fifty yards short of the stable and dismounted alongside the corral nearest the road. Bellows tied his scruffy paint to a post and leaned against the top rail, watching.

The ground back there had been chewed up by hooves and stank of manure in the hot sun. Across the afternoon quiet came the raucous honking of the mules and the shouts and curses of the mule skinners who were trying to sort them out. The near corral was empty; most of the activity was in the second corral, and the back corral looked to be for the animals chosen for the expedition. The skinners were running the mules into it through a chute, and those back there were already being outfitted with pack-saddles. Slocum saw a blue-uniformed sentry eyeing them from the front of the stable, but Bellows was intent on the men in the corrals.

"There they are," he said. "In that second corral

back. The two wearing buckskins. Jones is the one
with the mule. The tall one calls himself Ehrler.''

Slocum saw two men about his own age, wearing
fringed buckskins, both of them bearded and long-
haired like Bellows. One of them was leading a mule
around by the halter while the other, standing with a
bunch of troopers, looked for flaws in its gait.

Bellows started climbing the corral fence. "I'll
brace Ehrler. He's the one makes the decisions in
that pair. You just keep Jones off my back.''

"Hold it a minute," Slocum said. "We got trouble coming right here.''

The sentry had left his post in front of the stable
and was approaching along the ditch toward them,
carrying a rifle up at port arms. He looked young
enough to be a raw recruit and wore a nearly new
uniform, but the look in his eyes said he knew where
his duty lay.

"You'll have to get away from here," he said.
"This here area's restricted. Nobody's allowed here
but what's part of the expedition.''

"I got business in there," Bellows said.

"I'm sorry, sir. You can't go in there.''

Bellows dropped back to the ground. "Are you
going to stop me?''

"If you try, I guess I'll have to.''

Bellows didn't waste any time. He made as if to
go for his knife and feinted toward the sentry, dodging in low. Startled, the sentry brought the rifle
down. Bellows grabbed it by the barrel and jammed
it back into the kid's belly. The kid went down on
his rear with a sound like a cow belching up a cud.
His eyes bulged a bit, and for a second or two he

worked at getting air. Then he clutched his belly and rolled onto his side, retching into the weeds.

Bellows jacked the shells out of the rifle and threw them across the road. "Sonny, don't never try to bluff out your betters. There's things you ain't learned yet. Come on, Slocum." He dropped the rifle in the ditch and climbed up over the corral fence.

Slocum followed him, dropping down into the corral on the other side, looking back once to see the kid up on his knees, bent over, his hands still clutching his belly.

Jones and Ehrler saw them coming when they climbed the fence into the second corral. Jones turned the mule over to one of the troopers and turned to face them, waving his hat at another bunch of mules to shy them out of the way. The troopers traded glances and backed away a bit. Likely they figured, from the way Bellows was dressed, that this was something between him and Jones and Ehrler. Slocum hoped they stayed of that mind.

Bellows waded through the herd, never slackening his pace, pushing mules aside until he reached the cleared circle where the other two stood. Both of them wore pistols strapped up high around their waists; the tall one, Ehrler, had a knife in a sheath on the other side. If Slocum knew men of this stripe, likely the other one had a knife somewhere, too.

Bellows halted about ten feet away from them, his hands on his hips. "Well, boys, I see you found some honest work."

Ehrler glanced around at the troopers, but they showed no inclination to back him up. "Now, Clay," he said, "you don't know how things was."

"I know how things was," Bellows said. "You and Jones there was supposed to collect our pay and have it ready for me when I brought that last load of game into the reservation. Only, when I got there, you was gone. That's how things was."

"We waited for you, Clay," Jones said. "You didn't show up. We figured you'd run afoul of a bear or something."

"Shit," Bellows said. "The bear's never been born that could kill me. And you waited a hell of a long time. Overnight, they told me. And that was only so you could get in a good drunk."

"Now, Clay—" Ehrler said.

"Now, Clay, hell. I want my money," Bellows said.

Ehrler spread his hands wide. "It's gone, Clay. We're as broke as you are."

"You expect me to believe that?"

"Believe it or don't, it's true. Why else you think we signed on here as mule skinners? You know working mules ain't my favorite occupation."

Slocum sensed a cluster of mules milling toward him from his left. Without taking his eyes off Jones, he shooed them away with his hat. He could hear more mules and more troopers behind him, but he would just have to trust that the troopers would follow the lead of those in front of him. If they stayed out, he figured Bellows could handle Ehrler. And Jones would be no problem. Neither of these men was a gunfighter.

Bellows started advancing on Ehrler. Ehrler slipped the big Bowie knife out of its sheath and backed away. "You don't want to do this, Clay."

"The hell I don't," Bellows said, and drew his own knife.

Jones cast a quick glance at Slocum, and what he saw evidently kept his hand off his gun. When he went for a knife in a sheath hanging from a string down the back of his neck, Slocum slipped the Colt from its holster and waved him back.

"Playing with knives is not my style," he said. "You better just sit this one out."

Jones stopped with the string pulled halfway out. Then he let it drop back down his collar and edged to one side. Ehrler and Bellows were circling slowly, watching each other's eyes, knives flicking out like snakes' tongues. The troopers had herded the mules back, something like greed on their faces. Maybe it wasn't their fight, but watching it brought their blood up.

Ehrler feinted once and stepped in close, the knife slicing toward Bellows's gut. Bellows sidestepped to miss it and caught Ehrler's ankle with one moccasined foot, kicking the man's leg from under him. Ehrler hit the ground and tried to roll away. With a whoop like an Indian, Bellows was on him before he could recover, grabbing him by the hair and wrestling him around until he had him by the legs in a scissors grip, his knife pressed across Ehrler's throat. Ehrler struggled a bit, his own knife still in his hand, but the feel of that blade across his jugular quieted him down awfully quick.

"Where's my money?" Bellows demanded.

"It's gone, Clay," Ehrler gasped. "We lost it. Got in a faro game. We got cleaned out."

Still holding his knife across Ehrler's throat, Bellows cut a glance toward Slocum. "Search that other one. Turn his pockets out and see if there's any money."

Jones was fidgeting like he wanted to fight the air around him, but the sight of Slocum's Colt held him where he was. Slocum waved it at him. "You heard the man."

"He's telling the truth," Jones protested. "We lost it all in a faro game."

"Turn your pockets out," Slocum ordered.

Jones gave him a resigned look and began turning out his pockets. He tossed a jackknife on the ground, a plug of chewing tobacco, a wad of string, a box of matches; from the other pocket came a sack of Golden Grain, some rolling papers, and a handful of change. Holding the Colt on him, Slocum went up to lift the man's pistol from its holster. Then he patted the pockets down to make sure they were empty.

"He's got no money on him, Clay."

"Search this one," Bellows said. "Rip his shirt open. He keeps his cash in a money belt."

Slocum stuck Jones's pistol down in his waistband and backed over to where Bellows held Ehrler pinned. He took Ehrler's pistol from its holster and added it to the other, then brought his own knife up from where he kept it in a boot sheath. Ehrler's helpless eyes strained to watch as he cut the laces up the length of the buckskin shirt, laying bare the money belt around the man's middle. He cut the laces of the belt and laid it on the ground and started going through its small pockets, pulling out what he found there.

"Fifteen dollars, Clay."

Bellows swore. He shoved Ehrler away from him

and rolled to his feet, bringing his own gun out now. "You scum. You hid it somewhere."

"Clay, I swear," Ehrler said. "We lost it in a faro game. You know I never keep no money except in that money belt. That's all we got till we get paid off here."

Bellows looked from Jones to Ehrler, who was on his feet now, dusting himself off. "So you really did gamble it all away. I ought to gut you like a rabbit."

"Clay, if I had it I'd pay you. I ain't got it."

"Company coming, Clay," Slocum said.

He had seen the small group from the time it had started back through the corrals from the stable: five uniformed troopers led by a lieutenant. When they got close, he saw that one of the troopers was the young sentry Bellows had tangled with at the road. The lieutenant jostled his way through the mules, eyes taking in the gun in Bellows's hand, and the knives and Slocum with his Colt out and two more guns stuck in his belt. The lieutenant looked no more than twenty-five, a shavetail fresh from back East.

"What's going on here?" he said.

"A private dispute," Bellows said. "None of your affair."

"You're in a restricted area," the lieutenant said. "That makes it the army's affair. And this man here says you assaulted him when he tried to keep you out."

Bellows sheathed his knife but kept his gun out. "Junior, I was doing the army's work when you were still sucking at your mama's tit. Use a little respect when you talk to me."

The lieutenant looked him up and down. "Are you employed by the army?"

"Not now. Your army paid me out when it decided it had no use for me any more. So don't go thinking you can pull some regulation on me. I'm a free man, and I aim to stay that way."

"Then, if you have your private dispute taken care of, I suggest you leave. And stay away from this place. This is no regular army bivouac, it's a high-security area, and these corrals are under my command. If I see you here again, I'll report you to the local authorities. If the army can't deal with you, they can."

"I'll keep it in mind." Bellows holstered his pistol and turned back to Slocum. "Where's that money?" He took five dollars from the little roll and threw the rest on the ground at Ehrler's feet. "There. I'll take my share of that. If you was honest, you'd have brought it to me, faro game or no faro game. Both of you keep out of my way from now on. If I run onto you again, I just may take the rest of it out of your hides. Slocum, give them back their pistols and come on. The smell here's beginning to get to me."

Back at the road, Slocum mounted his bay and waited until Bellows had untied the paint and led it out across the ditch. Clay was still fuming. "Man can't even trust his partners any more. Five dollars for three months' work." He stuck a moccasined foot in the stirrup and swung up into the saddle. "We won't be going market hunting, that's for sure. What was that other thing you were talking about?"

"It's pretty complicated. And it's something I'm not sure it's smart to get involved in."

"How much does it pay?"

"If we do it—and if we pull it off—fifty thousand dollars."

Bellows reined the paint abruptly, staring at Slocum's face as if to see if he'd heard right. Eyebrows raised, he let out a slow whistle. "Let's get away from here," he said. "Let's go somewhere we can talk."

5

Half an hour later they were sitting on the edge of the boardwalk on the north side of the station square, watching a detail of troopers unload gear and supplies from the train which had brought the Arthur party into town. It was just past four o'clock by Slocum's pocket watch, and the hot August sun was still baking the square. Slocum had smoked the last of his cheroots and had his makings out now, rolling up a cigarette. Beside him, Bellows was honing his knife on a whetstone gripped between his knees.

"You figure this colonel's legitimate?" Bellows asked.

"I think he's in the army, all right, and a high-ranking officer. I think he believes what he says about Arthur. And it's for sure he wants the job done. I've got two thousand dollars in my pocket to prove it."

He touched a match to the cigarette and returned the makings to his pocket. From across the wide, dusty street came the hoarse bellow of the sergeant in charge of the unloading detail. Uniformed sentries were pacing the ground below the station platform, and two more were perched atop the train. The army was going to make getting at Arthur very difficult, and Slocum still wasn't sure he wanted any part of this.

"It's true what he told you about Arthur," Bellows said. "The way he got to be big chief back in Washington. I heard about that. Man before him was named Garfield. Got himself shot by somebody claiming to be on Arthur's side of things."

"You heard more than I did, then. I put all that behind me when I left Georgia. I don't care what they do back there. But if a man sets another one to kill his boss so he can take his job, it don't make sense for the man doing the killing to admit the reason for it."

"Can't tell about a man like that," Bellows said. "Maybe Arthur's people couldn't keep him controlled. Look at the man that killed Lincoln. Made no bones about what he was doing it for, and he was part of a conspiracy. I figure a man that would take on a job like that, shooting down the biggest man in the country—cold, no provocation—he's got to be a little touched."

"And here we are talking about taking on the same kind of job."

"We wouldn't be hiring on to *kill* him. Just to get him and turn him over to your colonel—and whoever's backing the colonel."

"The man's the head of the government," Slocum said. "That's not the way you change governments in this country. Not if I remember my school lessons right."

"If what the colonel says is true, the man's President because he hired somebody to kill the real one. And forcing a confession out of him might be the only way to put the government straight. God knows how they run things back in Washington. I've seen so many crooked government people out here, Indian agents and such, I'd believe anything." Bellows tested the knife blade with a finger, then went back to honing it on the whetstone. "Why'd he say they wanted it done out here?"

"Afraid if they tried anything back East, it might leak out and turn the country on its ear. If they can get a confession here, with Arthur up in the mountains, no communications coming out, they'll have time to prepare the country for it."

"Well, I'm for it," Bellows said. "I ain't never had the chance to make so much money before, and I won't ever again. And our part of the job's pretty simple. Get close to Arthur, grab him, and turn him over. Once we're paid off we can head for far country. Just in case things go wrong later, though I don't look for them to. If this colonel's like you say, he must have some pretty powerful people backing him up. They know how to control things."

Slocum watched a mule skinner lead a string of twenty pack mules into the square from around the far corner, but his mind was working on the colonel's plan. He still didn't like it. For one thing, impressive as the colonel was, Slocum didn't trust him, and when he didn't trust a man, generally sooner or later he discovered he'd had good cause. And this wasn't the kind of thing he favored putting his hand to. Too many faceless men lurking in the background, with characters and motives he had no way of judging. And the idea of toppling the biggest man in the government set his teeth on edge, even if he had long ago stopped considering it his government.

It wasn't the danger. He'd done things as difficult and dangerous before, but he'd been hoping to put that life behind him. That, besides the money, was the one positive point. The colonel had said those charges still outstanding against him would be dropped if he agreed to go along. And while he didn't like the threat implied in the offer, it would be good to have those things off his back. Once this was done, he could start clean.

"Well, I guess we can't afford to turn it down," he said. "Not for that much money, and us dead broke like we are. First thing is, we got to get ourselves attached to the expedition. The colonel doesn't even know exactly where they're going."

Bellows nodded toward the train station across the square, where the work detail was transferring gear and supplies from the piles along the platform to the packsaddles of the mules. "Could have signed on as mule skinners, but I guess I fouled that up. I'd have a hard time working alongside Jones and Ehrler, and likely that lieutenant wouldn't hire us now anyway. Why we got to sign on? We could just track them. Keep tabs on where they are and do it when the time seemed right."

"They'll be traveling with a cavalry escort. Seventy-five troopers. They'll have scouts and outriders for sure. It wouldn't be two days before we were spotted. And we have to be in close. It's not enough to know where they are. We've got to know where they're going next. The colonel wants it done where he can have his people set to take over."

"If they're going up into that Yellowstone country, we could hire on as guides. I know that country like it was mine."

"They've got guides. Besides, the colonel's already arranged it. You can guess that a bunch of Easterners coming out here on a spree wanted to bring some fancy women along. Some of the colonel's backers must be close to Arthur's crowd in Washington—because they wangled the job of supplying the women. Shipped a madam and some of her girls up here from Chicago. We'll be guiding them.''

"Thought you said they already got guides."

"For the main party. They'll travel separate from the women till they're away from civilization. Otherwise, the newspapers might get wind of it. Wouldn't do to have folks know there were whores along on the President's vacation.''

Bellows tested the knife blade against his finger again, then wiped it on his pants leg. "I always wanted to run me a whorehouse. This may be the closest I ever get. Remind me to thank the colonel when I meet him. Where are these women, and when do we get started?''

"Some big cattle buyer from Chicago has a ranch up here somewhere. He was the go-between when the arrangements were made. They're staying at his house out on the south edge of town. I got to tell the colonel we're going along. Then we're supposed to go meet the madam.''

Bellows grinned. "First thing I guess we better do is get us a bath and maybe a haircut. I can't go squiring the ladies looking like this." He put the knife back in its sheath, looking off toward the station platform, where a second string of pack mules had replaced the first. "I hope Jones and Ehrler have a good time wrassling them mules. Our job sounds a whole lot more pleasurable.''

6

The late sun was throwing long shadows across the street by the time they headed out toward the house in which the madam and her girls were staying.

Most of the crowd Slocum had seen earlier in the day were gone. A few drunks wandered the boardwalks, and several hangers-on still lingered in front of Arthur's hotel, but the town was quiet, the dusty streets hushed in that pale early evening light. A hot bath had brought Bellows out of his hangover; he'd had his hair and beard trimmed and had doused himself with some scent recommended by the barber, and was lounging along in the saddle whistling to himself like a youngster on his way to a square dance. Slocum still felt a little uneasy about what he'd agreed to do, but the decision was made, and he was trying to put the doubts behind him. The hot bath had helped—that, and the first set of new clothes he'd bought in nearly a year.

They had just emerged out into open country when they saw the house, about two hundred yards past the last few buildings at the edge of town. It was a big square building with an oddly truncated roof, set in a clump of trees off to the left of the road up ahead. Screened-in porches reached around both stories, and more trees dotted the front yard. Slocum brought the bay to a halt and scanned the grounds. There was a barn and a set of corrals in the rear and two buggies sitting unhitched around the back corner of the house, but the place looked deserted, the shutters drawn. From behind the barn came the bawling of a cow or two, but no other sound broke the evening quiet.

Bellows reined up beside him, the paint switching at flies. "Quite a house," he said.

"Man named Harrison owns it," Slocum said. "That cattle buyer I told you about. The colonel says he's not here. Brought the women to Green River and turned the house over to them and went back to Chicago. Guess he wants to keep clear of things."

"The women are keeping out of sight too. Place looks empty. This madam know what we've hired on to do? I mean, other than guiding her up into the back country?"

"She knows. She's not a part of it, except as a way of getting us close to Arthur, but she knows. Calls herself Mrs. Ryan. Harrison evidently trusts her to keep her mouth shut." He watched the house for a moment or two longer, but there was still no sign of life. "Well, let's go see what we got to deal with."

They turned into the lane leading to the house and reined up at a side door that looked to be the main entrance, though there was a set of steps leading to the screened-in porch in front. Slocum's rap brought a girl to the door. She was about twenty-five, small and slim and dark, wearing a high-collared dress which was tight and flashy enough to reveal her for what she was. She was prettier than most of the whores he'd encountered, almost elegant, despite the way that tight dress clung to her shapely little body.

"I'm John Slocum," he said. "This is Clay Bellows. We're here to see Mrs. Ryan."

The girl had the door open just a crack, as if to block the entrance. She might look elegant, but her voice had the Chicago streets in it. "You got an appointment?"

"Colonel Smith sent us."

A quick, practiced look sized them up, and she stepped back out of the doorway. "You can go in there," she said. "In the sittin' room. I'll fetch Mrs. Ryan." She flashed them that look again and started up a narrow staircase directly behind the door.

Slocum crossed the small foyer into what he figured was the sitting room. It was a large room, neat and sparsely furnished, with no rugs on the floor. A lot of light was coming in from somewhere, though he couldn't see any windows.

Beside him, Bellows whistled, impressed. "Rich man's house, for sure."

"We do this thing right," Slocum said, "you can buy your own."

Now he saw where the light was coming from. There was no ceiling in the room, at least not until it reached the roof, and there was a skylight up there, something he'd seen only once before in his life, in a whorehouse in New Orleans. Except for the sparse neatness and a set of longhorns mounted over a fireplace to the left of the door, the whole room reminded him of that New Orleans whorehouse, with the same wide stairway climbing up to a pillared veranda that went all the way around the upper floor. The whorehouse had had the same kind of furniture too—like the small settee against the far wall, with its ornately carved legs curving down into what looked like little claw feet.

"Strange what a rich man'll spend his money on," Bellows said.

"If he knows our Mrs. Ryan," Slocum said, "he's probably spent some of it on her. And if he's any example, she must have high-priced clients."

He was about to take a seat on one of the spindly chairs facing the settee when he heard footsteps approaching along an upstairs hallway. He looked up to see a tall, stately woman descending the stairs in a long, flowing gown. Her shoulders were bare beneath a mass of dark red hair that hung in ringlets below her ears. She crossed to the settee and offered her hand.

"I'm Mrs. Ryan," she said. "Gloria tells me you were sent by Colonel Smith."

Slocum introduced himself. "This is my partner, Clay Bellows," he said, intrigued to see the woman giving him the same frank once-over he was giving her. She was no longer young, but she was still beautiful, tall and statuesque, the gown cut deep enough to reveal the cleft between her large breasts. She smiled when she saw where his eyes were and turned to take a tray of drinks from the girl who had let them in. She set the tray on a small table in front of the settee and sent the girl from the room.

"Gloria doesn't know your real reason for being here," she said. "None of the girls do. I don't suppose they'd reveal it, but this way is safer for everyone, including them." She seated herself on one of the spindly chairs and waved them toward the settee. "Please have a drink and tell me something about yourselves. If we're going to be working together, I think we should get to know one another."

Slocum was less interested in telling her about himself than he was in learning something about her. The way her eyes glanced off his every time he looked at her made him want to get to know her a lot better. And he was having a hard time not looking, especially at those big breasts swelling above the cut of the gown. He recognized the impulse. He was still troubled by what he was getting himself into, and that always made him want to drown himself in a woman. A woman in bed could make a man forget what ailed him for a while.

He sampled the drink. It was very good whiskey, neat, in a man-sized glass. "I'd like to know what brought you into this," he said. "Why you agreed to go along."

She shrugged, her eyes meeting his and flicking away. "Curiosity. A sense of history, maybe. And a large amount of money."

Slocum believed the money part of it, but he figured it was likely Harrison had some sort of hold over her. With connections all the way back to Washington, Harrison must be a pretty big man, even in a place like Chicago. Likely she had to cooperate with him just to stay in business.

"How many girls did you bring?" Bellows asked.

"They wanted four. We won't be supplying entertainment for the whole party, after all. Just a few."

Slocum watched her breasts move heavily under the gown as she shifted in the chair. Whatever she was wearing under there, it wasn't much. "The colonel says Harrison was your go-between, but he's gone back to Chicago. Who's your liaison with Ar-

thur's people? We're going to have to learn their
itinerary.''

"A Lieutenant Troy has been assigned to see
we're taken care of. He was sent out here in advance
and has been making arrangements. We're to leave
ahead of the main party, traveling separately to a
place called Fort Washakie, somewhere north of
here. We'll be told there where we're going next.
No one's to know we're attached to the expedition,
you understand.''

"They'll never keep it a secret from their own
people," Slocum said. "All those troopers and mule
skinners will know."

"I understand we're to camp somewhat away from
the main party even after we've joined them,"
she said. "Everything's supposed to be kept very
discreet."

"Discreet or not, it'll never work," Slocum said.
"But that's their problem."

"Yes," she said. "I suppose it is. Lieutenant
Troy says we'll be traveling by mule-drawn wagons.
Not a very appetizing prospect. And I don't know
this country at all. Can you give me some idea of
what we'll be faced with?"

Bellows exchanged a glance with Slocum. "Trail's
not too bad from here to Fort Washakie. Depends on
where they go after that. If we're going up into
Yellowstone country like I hear, it could get pretty
rough. That's mountain country. Hard on wagons."

Slocum heard stifled giggles and the rustle of
dresses on the veranda above him. Mrs. Ryan looked
up, annoyed, but obviously amused too. "All right,"
she said. "If you're going to flutter around up there,
you might as well come down and be introduced."

The girls came scampering down the stairs, led by the slim dark-haired Gloria, holding up their long skirts to keep from tripping. Almost prim in what likely were their going-out-in-society dresses, blushing and still stifling giggles, they ranked themselves alongside Mrs. Ryan's chair, each one stepping forward and dipping into a little curtsey as she was introduced: a bright-eyed, busty blonde named Judy; a tall, leggy creature whose red hair made her look a little like Mrs. Ryan and who was called Hope; and another brunette named Angela. Likely they were the cream of Mrs. Ryan's brood. They were all prettier than any soiled doves Slocum had seen from Montana to Mexico, and they seemed a lot livelier, too—girlish and flirtatious in a way that wasn't just professional. It was only when he saw their excited eyes taking in his gun and his boots and spurs and Bellows's buckskins and Bowie knife that he figured out why. These were city girls, likely on their first trip west of the Mississippi, and what they knew about this country could only have come from dime novels about the Wild West. Likely he and Bellows were as exotic to them as armored knights.

"All right, girls," Mrs. Ryan said. "Back upstairs. And stay in your rooms. I have business to discuss."

With excited backward glances, the girls scurried up the wide stairway. Slocum heard their giggles receding along an upstairs hall. When they were gone, Mrs. Ryan turned to Bellows. "Now," she said. "You were telling me what we might expect."

"Yes, ma'am," Bellows said. "I wouldn't worry none about Indians, if that's bothering you. The army's got the hostiles pretty much rounded up in this territory. And, like I said, it depends on where we're going. Worst thing is, you'll be uncomfortable. Covering that much country by wagon, especially in the mountains, you'll wish you'd stayed in Chicago.''

"Lieutenant Troy told me we'll be sleeping in tents.'' Mrs. Ryan flicked that amused glance at Slocum, her eyes lingering just a bit longer than they might have. "Well, I did see this as something of an adventure. I suppose we'll endure it. And it will give me something to remember in my old age.''

"This lieutenant say where the transportation's coming from?'' Slocum asked.

"The army is supplying everything. Two wagons—escort wagons, he called them—four mules for each wagon, supplies, and provisions. He came by to see me this afternoon, after the colonel sent word you were coming. I told him you'd be in contact with him as soon as possible. Since we'll be traveling a separate route, we have to leave before the President's party in order to arrive on time.''

"We'd better contact him tonight, then,'' Slocum said. "If I know the army, it'll take a while to requisition all that stuff.''

"You'll find him in town, at the Hotel Meyers,'' she said. "Which reminds me, I don't know where you're staying, but I'd like you to move in here, if you will. This house has sufficient room, and my girls are feeling uneasy. This country is all very strange to them, and they don't like being alone without protection. We've all heard too many stories about the West—the shootings and the desperadoes. I'm sure we'd all feel safer with two men in the house, men of the West, who would know how to handle things.''

Slocum wondered what she would say if she knew he'd spent last night sleeping in a stable and Bellows had passed out in a dirty storeroom back of a saloon. He wasn't going to turn the offer down. ''I figure that's part of our job,'' he said. ''We'll be spending the next month together in pretty close quarters. The sooner we get used to being in each other's way, the better.''

''That brings up a delicate subject,'' Mrs. Ryan said. ''Since we will be spending all that time together, in such close quarters. I think it was obvious the girls are intrigued by you, the first genuine plainsmen they've actually met. I won't have that taken advantage of. Forgive me for being blunt, but that's part of *my* job. Each of these girls is here by choice. She is what she is, but I won't have a man forcing himself on her.'' She smiled now, her eyes giving Slocum that frank once-over again. ''However, if any of them takes a fancy to either of you, I won't interfere. I did promise them adventure and, given the discomfort we're obviously going to have to endure, they deserve whatever adventure they can find out here.''

From the looks she'd been giving him, Slocum wondered if she herself wasn't a little intrigued by the first genuine plainsman she'd actually met—if that was what she wanted to call him. ''Ma'am,'' he said, ''I think you'll find that we're gentlemen. I've never handled a situation like this before, and I know Clay here hasn't, either, but we're not the kind to force ourselves on anybody.''

''Thank you,'' she said. ''I thought I'd judged

you right. And please don't call me 'ma'am.' Call me Laura. And now, if you'd like, I can show you around the house. You can each choose a room to sleep in.''

Slocum had other ideas. All those looks he'd been getting from her, the hints about adventure and intriguing plainsmen, the obviously unfettered breasts under that loose gown—all that had him wanting a room for something other than sleeping. And, from the look in her eye, he suspected she knew it.

"We had better contact that Lieutenant Troy first," he said. "Clay, why don't you ride in and find him? See how soon we can pick up what we need."

Bellows was just finishing his drink. His eyes cut to Slocum over the rim of the glass, and he barely managed to stifle a grin. He hadn't missed what had been going on here. He downed the last of the whiskey and retrieved his floppy hat from his knee. "Pick me out any old place," he said. "I sleep just as well on the floor. But don't take too long about it. I ought to be back in a couple of hours."

When the side door closed behind him, Mrs. Ryan smiled at Slocum and rose from her chair. "Come," she said, "I'll show you the bedrooms."

7

Upstairs, Slocum followed Laura Ryan along the open veranda and into the east wing of the house. The hallway, like the sitting room, had a long skylight in the ceiling. Typical Easterner's indulgence, Slocum thought. A flat roof in country where the snow could pile up as high as a man's head. There had to be shutters to close over those skylights in winter, and that would leave the house dark as the grave. But likely Harrison didn't spend much time up here after the first snowfall. He was rich; he could winter where he pleased.

Laura opened a door off the right of the hall and ushered him into what had to be the master bedroom. It was very large, with a fireplace on one wall and a rank of windows along another, through which he could see the evening light stretching across the prairie. In the center of the room was the largest canopied bed he'd ever seen. He turned to see her leaning against the door, watching him.

"Quite a room," he said.

"It's my bedroom." She had her hands behind her, propped on the doorknob, and the way she was bent at the waist displayed those heavy breasts cradled in the bodice of her gown. "This is the room you wanted to see, isn't it?"

For the first time, with no attempt to disguise his interest, he let his eyes dwell on that statuesque body: the long legs rising up into womanly hips, the hollow in the gown where it crossed the juncture of her thighs, the slender waist above which those breasts seemed so prominent. "If it's your bedroom, it's the room I wanted to see."

"I thought so." She crossed the room to stand only touching distance away, placing her hands flat against his chest, head down, so he couldn't see her eyes. "Are you sure you're not being—shall we say diplomatic? There are four girls in this house, young and pretty, any one of whom would take you into her bed in a minute. The gunfighter or outlaw or whatever you are, since you're working for the colonel—the adventure she could boast about to her friends in Chicago. Why me? I'm thirty-nine years old."

"So am I. We're alike, you and me. We're both working for the colonel. I don't usually get looks like you've been giving me from a woman in your profession. And, given a choice, I've always preferred a woman to a girl."

She had brought her hands down to caress the gunbelt draped around his hips, watching her slim fingers as if fascinated by what they touched. "I'm glad," she said. "You can't know how bored I am by the men who choose to associate with me. There's something about wealth and society and politics which makes a man fat in his soul—makes him not a man." Now her eyes came up to meet his, something like heat rising in them. "You're lean and hard. I like that. I've heard men out here are different. Is that true, Mr. Slocum?"

He pulled her abruptly up against him and closed his mouth on hers, feeling those big breasts swelling against his chest. He could hear her breathing quicken as her warm wet tongue found his, circling, pressing, seeking. She broke the kiss then, her heavy-lidded eyes looking up at him, her lower body pressing against that hardness at his groin.

"I guess you do desire me, don't you?"

For answer he pulled her around against a pillar of the bed's canopy and ripped the gown from her shoulders, stripping her abruptly to the waist, her breasts bobbing out, big and flushed and bare.

Her gaze was locked on his face but seemed somehow at the same time focused on her own nakedness, as if she could see herself through his eyes. She clutched the gunbelt at his hips, her groin still pressed up against his, her upper body arched back against the canopy pillar, breasts rising and falling with her quickened breathing. The sight of her had made his throat go dry; he cupped his hands around the back of her neck, slowly slid them down her warm satiny shoulders, down her upper arms, bringing them slowly around to cradle those large heavy breasts in his palms. She began to tremble as he ran his callused palms up across her stiff nipples, his hands circling each breast, soft and slow. She rocked her hips into his, pressing harder against that hardness beneath his jeans.

"I may run a house," she said, "but I'm not, as you say, a woman 'in the profession.' I'm a lady, Mr. Slocum. I run a salon where men may come to loosen their collars and be what their wives will not allow them to be. I am not a whore, and I have never been a whore. I have my own needs. I promised myself I'd find a man on this trip to satisfy those needs.''

She was moving with every stroke of his hands, arching up to meet the rough touch of his palms on her breasts, head tilting slowly to the side as he slid his hand up the side of her neck. Her eyes were watching his face, and again he had the impression that she could tell by his look what the touch of her made him feel. Now he slid his hands down and found a hook at the side of the gown, released it, and watched the gown drop to the floor.

She eased it aside with one slippered foot and stood naked before him, legs spread, hands still gripping his hips, eyes still locked on his. She might be thirty-nine, but she hadn't lost her shape; it was only thickened a bit by that padding which came to a woman in her prime. The legs were still long and shapely, the hips firm, her belly with only that slight rise that distinguished a woman from a girl, her waist slender but soft under his hands, her breasts large as cannon shells but proud and full, settled only a bit into womanly ripeness.

Now she brought her hands up and began unfastening the buttons of his shirt.

He had the presence of mind to kick off his boots, but he let her do the rest, unwilling to take his hands off that smooth, satiny skin, molding her figure with the swoop and glide of his palms like a sculptor shaping clay. He heard his gunbelt hit the floor with a thump. Then her fingers were working at his trousers. She watched his eyes as she tugged them down and he stepped out of them, the air suddenly cool against his skin, naked as she was. She gripped his hips again and arched up against him, but she was dry and tight, not open to entry. Something in her look told him that she would not like gentleness; he found himself with one hand and forced himself in, ramming through flesh clenched tight as a fist, and saw her flinch with something that was more than pain, something fierce but welcoming.

For a moment they stood that way, she on wide-spread tiptoe, trembling, him sunk deep up between her thighs. He began to move, holding her by the waist, working out and in, still resisted by that un-yielding inner grip that clenched him like a fist. She ducked her head, looking down past those quivering breasts to where he plunged and retreated, thrust and withdrew, but he could still sense something tight and controlled in her arms, in her hips, a lack of response to his movement, and that brought anger up in him. He slowed, thrusting in slow and deep, watching what he could see of her face to judge where she was. She was avoiding his gaze; he knew it, though he couldn't see her eyes—something about the angle of her head, half canted away, told him she was still resisting, and that made anger rise up hotter within him, and it was only when the anger made him forget her, sent him lost into his own heat, made him care no longer about her at all but only about that slow surge of pleasure climbing, it seemed, up into his very innards that her head came slowly up and he saw the heat in her eyes that told him she had reached the place she needed to be. He felt her become moist now, moist and slippery. And now her hips began to flex with a power of their own, re-sponding to her own inner feeling.

Her eyes were locked on his now, fierce and hot and full of something itself near to anger, her breath coming in ragged shudders as she rocked and lunged to meet his thrusts. And now her fingernails sank into his flesh, ten tiny little knives of pain that brought him to a point where he could no longer stand.

He worked to find voice enough to say, *"On the bed,"* but she didn't move, didn't take her eyes from his, her fingernails sinking in deeper. *"On the bed,"* he said fiercely, and when she still didn't move, he pushed her away from the pillar and tumbled her back onto the wide mattress.

He landed in her so hard she cried out. He braced himself and drove up into her again, forcing her up onto the bed. That only seemed to excite her more; her long legs came up into the air, knees bent, spread wide and sagging apart; her arms went up behind her head and gripped the coverlet, clutching it as if to save her life. Her back was arched, her huge breasts bobbling and jiggling as their bodies writhed and rocked in a rhythm that had become one.

But she wasn't going to make it; he felt her begin to balk, felt that rigid control begin to set in to her body again, that stubborn resistance he'd felt before. He ran his hands up under her shoulders to seize the hair at the back of her head, forcing her eyes to meet his, slowing again to catch that lost rhythm, finding it, bringing it back up, holding her imprisoned by her hair till he could tell by the look in her eyes that she was near again—rising, writhing, something like fear on her face, fear that she would lose it again. When he felt her reaching again toward that peak, he brought his hot mouth down close beside her throat and whispered fiercely in her ear: *"Come, come, whore . . . ,''* and was rewarded by the guttural cry suddenly wrenched from her throat, by the violent eruption that seized her like a death throe, her hips working fast and frantically as she cleared that last hurdle, bringing him with her, bucking and lunging, shuddering up and quivering in mid-air, falling back to the bed only to quiver violently up again, all resistance broached and broken and bursting out of her like a river through a shattered dam. And when she lay trembling on the coverlet, unable any more to rise, he brought his mouth down on hers to quench her cries, his hands curved around the nape of her neck, her breasts cradled in the embrace of his upper arms.

She quivered and trembled for what seemed a full five minutes at least, her legs locked around the small of his back. Then her eyes came up to meet his, large and liquid, but there was still something intense there, something that would not give. For a long while she searched his eyes with her own, slowly stroking his chest. Then she rolled slowly onto her side, the grip of her thighs still holding him inside her, but her legs coming down now so that her ankles were hooked behind his. Her long, slim fingers continued to trace those parts of his body she could reach, and she was studying his face as if she had added cause now to discover if he was the man she thought he was.

"You're good," she said finally. "I sensed you'd be good, and you are."

He couldn't restrain a faint smile. It wasn't every day he was told that by a woman who likely knew every kink and twist in half a thousand men, no matter what she'd said. He could tell by the look on her face that she wasn't going to mention those words he'd used to bring her over. That was private, secret, something that didn't exist as long as she didn't acknowledge it. That was all right; bed talk didn't need repeating out of bed. She wasn't the first woman he'd sensed would respond to that kind of thing, and he knew enough to know she needed her own image of herself to keep her self-respect. And he believed what she'd said earlier, that she'd never been a whore—even that she was a lady. In her way, she was, and it was as a lady that she was able to run the kind of house she likely had in Chicago, the kind that attracted men like Harrison, men with money and political power. He liked what she'd said about men like that—that the wealth and the drive for power made them something less than men. He had never met a man like that, smug and stout in a suit and a vest, that he'd felt any respect for.

The thought brought the image of Chester Arthur to his mind, that portly figure on the station platform, who had perhaps hired the cold-blooded killing of another of his own kind to get to the position he held. It helped, thinking of him that way. Something less than a man, something that had to be dealt with, for reasons somebody else could vouch for. He would take their word for the reasons.

He was holding her in the crook of one arm, stroking the voluptuous slopes of her body with his free hand, watching her nipples bend and spring upward as he dragged his palm across them. "You're quite a woman," he said. "It's not every woman it can be that good with."

She smiled then, the first smile since they'd entered the bedroom. "I think I'm going to like you.

You seem to understand me. Most men are so concerned with themselves they can't see beyond a woman's skin. Not unless she's some fragile little thing afraid of her own shadow.''

"I never liked fragile women," he said.

"Good. I've never been a fragile woman. Though sometimes it can be nice to let one's hair down and not hold on so hard."

"In bed," he said. "Holding on hard's not good in bed. Necessary for living, maybe, but not for bed. A little letting go is good for you. Good for anybody.''

She touched a fingertip to his left nipple. "If they're fortunate enough to find someone capable of making it happen."

"Everybody makes it happen himself. You make it happen yourself. What's in your mind makes it happen."

She smiled again. " A man who thinks too, and can talk. I believe I'll enjoy this trip. Wagons and mules and discomfort and all. But right now I think we'd better get out of this bed before Mr. Bellows comes back."

What he thought was that she could sometimes be too superior to bear and that she needed a good cuff behind the ear. And that if she kept up that kind of talk, he was likely to give her one.

8

They left Green River the next day in the two escort
wagons provided by Lieutenant Troy, each drawn by
a four-mule team, the bay and the paint tied on
behind.

The wagons were good sturdy Studebakers, close
to 2,500 pounds lighter than the prairie schooners,
more maneuverable and better suited to the rough
country they would be crossing. They came already
loaded up with tents and supplies, the feed boxes
filled with grain for the mules, but as usual the army
had found a way to screw up. The wagon bodies still
bore the U. S. stamp with the crossed sabers of the
cavalry, complete with regimental number and troop
letter, and the same markings were stenciled on the
white canvas tops. Hardly the way to pass unnoticed, with the big 5 and G proclaiming to the world
that the wagons were from the troop escorting
President Arthur.

Slocum made a special trip into town to buy new,
unmarked canvas tops and some blue paint, match-
ing the color of the wagon bodies, to splash over the
markings on the sides. He had wanted to leave at
dawn, but it was early afternoon before they finally
pulled out of town and headed north. And he couldn't
even put the blame where tradition demanded, on the

women; they hadn't really unpacked since their arrival from Chicago, and all he had to do with them was to load their trunks aboard and see that they were comfortable.

There was a good road between Green River and Fort Washakie, and the three days' travel was relatively easy going. The army had supplied Sibley stoves to keep the tents warm at night, and the girls seemed to find the whole trip an adventure, oohing and aahing at the scenery and chattering enthusiastically about everything they saw. The lead wagon was rigged up to accommodate the girls. Mrs. Ryan usually sat on the driver's seat beside Slocum, and Billows drove the second wagon, which contained the bulk of the supplies.

"Don't hardly seem fair," Billows said the first time they stopped to give the mules a rest and some water. "All them fair maidens, and my friend Slocum here keeps 'em all to himself. All I got to look at is the back end of a couple span of mules."

"Be grateful for small favors," Slocum said. "At least the army's given you a seat to sit on. A few years back, when you had to guide these teams from a saddle on the near wheeler, you'd have been riding one of them mules."

"Riding a mule's not what I had in mind," Billows said, "if you get my meaning."

Slocum couldn't suppress a grin at Billows's complaint, but he himself soon began to tire of the chatter of the girls, and he wasn't sorry when, on the morning of the second day out, dark-haired Gloria elected to ride with Billows on the wagon in the rear. There were three tents—one for Mrs. Ryan, one for the girls, and one for Slocum and Billows—

but Slocum had spent the night with Mrs. Ryan, so he figured Gloria's move meant Bellows had convinced her to move into the tent with him.

Bellows had made himself popular with all the girls, telling tall tales around the campfire about his exploits with Indians and grizzlies and all manner of hair-raising escapes from death. For all Slocum knew, he might be trading girls every hour or so in that tent. But Bellows denied it when asked.

"Hell, one woman's enough for me," he said. "I ain't as young as I used to be. But I'm going to be sorry when we tie up with Arthur's bunch and I have to watch that girl start working her trade."

They reached Fort Washakie on the evening of the third day and set up camp about two miles from the fort, downstream on the Little Wind River. The President's party arrived by wagon- and pack-train the evening after they did, and Slocum rode in the next morning to meet with Lieutenant Troy, their liaison officer.

It was the first time Slocum had met Troy, and he didn't like the way the man treated him. He hadn't foreseen how taking on the job of guiding the women would make him look in the eyes of the man employing him, and he didn't enjoy being treated like the fancy man Troy evidently thought he was. But he bit his tongue to keep his temper. There was too much riding on this job for him to foul it up just for the satisfaction of closing Troy's mouth with his fist.

He had a drink at one of the saloons in the shanty town, which was exactly like the ones that surrounded all such forts. Then he made arrangements for re-supply at the post trader's store and left the fort on his bay. The man calling himself Colonel Smith had said he would rendezvous with him here, but though the place was crowded with Indians and teamsters and drifters he saw no sign of the colonel. But that wasn't his problem; if the colonel wanted him, he could take the trouble to look for him.

It was about two in the afternoon by the time he got back to camp. Laura Ryan was in her tent, but the girls were doing their laundry in an iron pot over the fire, and they had Bellows hauling fresh water up from the river.

"Damn fool women," Bellows said when Slocum dismounted. "Wanted to hang their stuff out to dry on the mules' picket line. Told 'em them mules'd eat half their wardrobes. A mule'll eat anything that don't look like it's alive. You find out where we're going?"

"The next leg of it, anyway," Slocum said. "We're going up into the Wind River range from here. Crossing the mountains into Jackson Hole."

Bellows set his buckets down. "Goddamn, that's a rough trip for wagons. But hell, these women wanted adventure. I guess they'll get it. Though maybe not the kind they expected."

Mrs. Ryan came out of her tent as Slocum was unstrapping a paper-wrapped parcel from the back of his cantle.

"I saw your friend Troy," he said, and began undoing the parcel. "These are for you and the girls. Poke bonnets. Got 'em at the post trader's store."

She turned one over in her hand and gave him a faintly ironic smile. "Poke bonnets? What are they for?"

"Indians are putting on a show for the President this afternoon. Thought you'd like to go watch it."

The girls crowded up around her, begging for the privilege. They hadn't yet seen an Indian, and they'd been wanting to go into the fort ever since they'd arrived.

"You think we should risk it?" she said. "We're supposed to keep our distance while we're here. What if someone connects us to the President's party?"

"You wear them poke bonnets and we all go in one wagon, won't nobody notice. Folks from the fort'll likely think we're a family party passing through on our way somewhere. Everybody else'll think you're officers' wives. You're going to need those bonnets out in this sun, anyway. We're going up into high country, and the sun gets mighty hot in that thin air."

When she finally agreed, the girls rushed to the tent for their paint and powder. Slocum had to do a little talking to get them to go barefaced. They had taken to leaving most of the paint off on the trip up, and those dusty dresses and the poke bonnets made them look a hell of a lot less like city women. He wanted to keep it that way.

He used the buckets of water to put out the fire while Bellows hitched up one of the wagons, and they set out for the fort with Bellows driving and Slocum riding the bay alongside. Mrs. Ryan was on the driver's seat beside Bellows, and the girls kept crowding up to look out the front, gazing wide-eyed at what Slocum figured to them was a scene from one of those dime novels, though to him it didn't look like much.

As forts went, Washakie was more hospitable than

most, but it was still just a sprawling assemblage of buildings. The streets of shanty town were dusty, and what stores there were were weather-beaten and dilapidated, with the squawking of chickens from the married non-coms' living quarters and the yapping of dogs that seemed to be a constant noise on every reservation he'd ever been on.

There was no stockade; the place had been built after the army had stopped stockading its forts, relying on large garrisons to deter Indian attack. Except for the barracks and the uniforms there wasn't much in the way of military smartness for anybody to see.

They passed through shanty town and up through the fort proper, past the officers' row and the parade ground and on out toward a flat plain north of the fort. A large crowd was already gathered to watch the show. Slocum's party had to pass along the back of the mob and work their way in through some other wagons at the far corner before they could get up close enough to see.

The crowd was bunched up behind a kind of reviewing stand, where the fort's staff had set up a row of folding canvas chairs for the President's party. The entire fort had turned out for the affair, soldiers and troopers and officers and wives, dotted here and there with civilian employees and people who'd come in from the surrounding territory to get a look at the President. Slocum could just make him out in the center of the row of chairs: a portly figure barely distinguishable from those around him. Troop G, his cavalry escort, was lined up in a single rank that stretched along the front of the crowd, their horses facing out onto the plain.

"Where are the Indians?" Gloria asked, craning her neck over Bellows's shoulder.

"Look out there," Slocum said.

A large cloud of dust was rising on the horizon. Out of the dust came a vast array of Indian ponies, several hundred braves spread out in a line across the plain, riding directly toward the crowd. The line seemed to dance and waver with color: calico ponies and paints, coupsticks and lances, feathered head-dresses and beaded buckskins, streaks of war paint on every face.

They had been coming at a trot. Now they kicked into a run, and Slocum could hear their whoops and yelps above the noise of the crowd. The girls set up a chorus of squeals, scrambling up to hold to the bows under the canvas top so they could see out over the driver's seat.

"My, they do look fearsome," Mrs. Ryan said. "What kind of Indians are they?"

"Shoshone and Arapaho," Bellows said, "but I wouldn't worry. These are reservation Indians, and they're tame. Most of 'em, anyway. The Shoshone have been friendly ever since Lewis and Clark passed through this country eighty years ago. Sacajawea, the Indian woman that guided Lewis and Clark up through the Rockies, she was a Shoshone."

Judy, the busty blonde, was hanging on to the front bow of the wagon top, watching wide-eyed as the Indians came on. "So there *are* good Indians," she remarked.

"Some'll tell you the only good Indian's a dead one," Bellows said, but "the Shoshone have never made war on whites. Washakie's been their chief for forty years, and maybe he's smarter than some, or maybe he could see the handwriting on the wall before some others could. Anyway, the Shoshone were on our side from the first, protecting wagon trains from other Indians, going after stolen stock and returning it. They even settled on this reservation without any fuss. "That don't mean they don't like to fight. Fighting and hunting's about all these Plains Indians live for. The Shoshone were fighting the Blackfoot and the Crow all the time they were friendly to us."

The Indians seemed about to ride the crowd down. They were coming in at a flat-out gallop, whooping and yelling, waving their coupsticks and rifles. At the last minute they pulled up with a flourish, skidding to a halt in a cloud of dust not more than twenty yards in front of the row of chairs. Two calico ponies came dancing out of the center of the line, their riders done up in beaded buckskins and feathered headdresses that hung down below their knees. An army officer sitting beside the President, most likely the fort's commandant, rose to greet them as they dismounted.

"One on the left's Coal Black, head man of the Arapaho," Bellows said. "The other's Washakie, chief of the Shoshone."

"Washakie?" Laura asked. "You mean the army named their fort after an Indian?"

"Yes, ma'am. Used to be Camp Brown, but they renamed it to honor the old man. He's quite an Indian. See that sash and the metal disk he's wearing around his neck? That's a medal he got from another President, back in 'Sixty-six. Johnson, I believe that was. And see that saddle on his pony? All them bright trimmings? That saddle's trimmed with silver. President Grant sent him that saddle. They gave it to him in real style, too, the troopers lined up in formation, bugles blowing, speeches, and everything. I was here to watch that one. In 'Seventy-six, that was.''

The President rose from his chair and was presented to the two chiefs. Slocum watched Washakie shake the President's hand, white-man's fashion, and then listen while the Great White Father said a few words Slocum couldn't hear and likely Washakie couldn't understand. The old chief looked as tall and straight as any of his braves, his long gray hair hanging unbraided to his shoulders, below the gold rings in his ears.

"He looks very fierce," Judy said.

"That's just 'cause he's got his finery on," Bellows said. "Usually he wears a floppy white man's hat and a bulky old coat with a blanket tied around his middle. But don't let that fool you. He's eighty-five years old, but he still rules this reservation like a king. Some time back, when he was about seventy, a few of the younger braves got to grousing that maybe the old man was getting too old and too soft to lead the tribe. So old Washakie went off on a little hunting trip all by himself. A man-hunting trip. Came back carrying seven fresh Blackfoot scalps. There hasn't been much talk against him since.''

The presentation ceremonies were over now, and the President returned to his chair. Coal Black and Washakie remounted and wheeled their ponies, and Washakie shook a gourd-shaped rattle at his braves. The Indian ponies started filing off to the right, rapidly kicking into a run that took them in a wide circle back out onto the plain. About a hundred yards out they turned left flank in as pretty a move as any cavalry regiment and reined up in a line facing south.

Now Troop G, the President's escort, started off in a similar file to the left. When they were about even with the line of Indians, they turned right flank and pulled to a halt, the two long ranks facing each other about two hundred yards apart.

Coal Black and Washakie were still sitting on their ponies in front of the President's party. Slocum saw the troopers hauling out their carbines, levering rounds into the chambers. The Indian ponies were dancing and shifting in anticipation, the braves shaking their coupsticks and waving their rifles in the air. In the center of the cavalry line, Troop G's bugler brought his bugle up.

"Well, I'll be damned," Bellows said. "You see what I'm seeing?"

"I see it," Slocum said. "I'm not sure I believe it. I just hope they got blanks in those rifles."

Above the noise of the crowd came the notes of the bugle blowing the call to charge. The two long lines leaped toward each other, horses stretching out at a run, the Indians yipping and yelping. The sound of rifle fire started sputtering across the plain.

"Look!" Gloria cried. "They're shooting at each other!"

"A battle," Bellows said. "A goddamn battle. Cavalry against Indians. It ain't been but seven years since Custer got his whole command wiped out, and here they are doing the same thing for show. There were Arapaho in that bunch at the Little Bighorn too. Could be one of them braves out there had a hand in killing old Yellowhair."

Even Mrs. Ryan had stood up to get a better look

now. The crowd was pressing in on both sides of the wagon, but all eyes were on the plain out in front, where those two lines were closing on each other in a rush, the braves yelling and swinging war clubs, the troopers firing in concentrated salvos. Slocum felt a horse nudge up against him and turned to see an army captain kneeing his mount up alongside the bay.

He was about to protest when the captain asked, "You John Slocum?"

The captain was watching the mock battle, not looking at Slocum. He looked more like a desk man than a field officer.

"I might be," Slocum said.

"I'm Captain Williams. Colonel Smith wants to see you back at the fort."

Slocum concealed his surprise. He hadn't expected to meet anybody else who was connected with this thing. But maybe there were people out here the colonel knew, people who would recognize him if he showed himself.

"How'd you know who I was?"

"You were pointed out to me earlier," the captain said. "Better make it quick. The colonel wants to be out of here before this show is over."

The battle out on the plain had become a wild melee. Indians and troopers were circling each other at a run, their horses cutting and darting through the dust as each side worked to show off its skill. The popping of the blanks sounded like firecrackers at a Chinese festival.

Slocum caught Bellows's eye and saw that he'd overheard. "Take care of the women," he said. "If I'm not back before this thing's over, I'll see you in camp.'' He edged his bay around and followed the captain off through the press of riders and wagons.

The noise of the crowd and the mock battle soon fell away behind, but the captain didn't say anything all the way back to the fort. Slocum was surprised to find them heading for officers' row. With everybody out watching the show, the place was deserted, but the fort was the last place he had expected to meet with the colonel. A rendezvous in camp—at night, say—would have been a lot safer. Maybe the colonel didn't want the women to get a look at him, but letting the women know who he was seemed to Slocum less risky than the possibility of being recognized by another officer.

Fort Washakie had been in existence long enough to have regular little houses for the married officers, with yards and shade trees. The captain led him along the back of the row and dismounted at the rear of a clapboard cottage.

''Leave your mount here,'' he said. ''We'll walk the rest of the way.''

Slocum tied his bay to the picket fence beside the other man's sorrel and followed the captain. Williams turned in at the gate behind a larger cottage and led him inside without knocking.

They passed through a dark kitchen and along a little hallway into a front parlor. The colonel was waiting by a window, dressed like a civilian, in a broadcloth suit and a wide-brimmed plainsman's hat big enough to shield his face if he pulled it down. Whoever he was, Slocum figured he was known at Washakie, and he didn't want to be recognized here.

The colonel greeted him with that broad diplomatic smile, as full of energy as ever and just as much the gracious host. "Glad to see you made it," he said. "Hope you had no trouble on the way. Captain, bring in some coffee. Sit down, Mr. Slocum, sit down."

The colonel took a chair opposite him, lighting up a cigar while the captain served the coffee. Slocum accepted a cigar and studied the room.

Though Williams hadn't knocked on the way in, he knew these weren't any captain's quarters. The army doled out living quarters by rank, starting with a single room for a second lieutenant, and he had counted the rooms on the way in. This place had five. It had to be the house of a lieutenant colonel. It was furnished with good quality tables and chairs and even had wallpaper, which had to have been shipped all the way from Chicago or San Francisco. Slocum figured whoever lived here had his family out watching the battle, but the colonel wouldn't have set up a meeting here without the occupant knowing it. He found himself wondering just how widespread the colonel's associates were.

The captain finished serving and went to stand at the window, where he could keep a lookout. The colonel sipped at his coffee, the saucer delicately balanced in one hand.

"You have a look at our Indian friends out there? I understand they're doing battle with Troop G just to entertain the President."

"Playing at battle, anyway," Slocum said. "Crazy Horse must be turning in his grave."

"Yes, Crazy Horse would never have done such a thing. Crazy Horse was a warrior—a brave man, but maybe not smart enough to see where he was headed." The colonel grinned. "Washakie, now—

Washakie understands politics. A brave man who understands politics can achieve a lot more than just a few bloody battles for the history books. And even Crazy Horse said Washakie was the greatest of the chiefs.'' He drew slowly on his cigar, watching Slocum with those keen eyes. "Let's get down to business. Have you seen your liaison with Arthur's party yet? Do you know where you'll be going?''

"I saw him this morning," Slocum said. "We're going northwest, leaving on the ninth—tomorrow. Going up into the Wind River range, across the continental divide and down the Gros Ventre River into Jackson Hole. I understand the President's party plans to spend some time there, hunting and fishing. Where we're going after that, I don't know. I won't know until they tell me, and my understanding is that I won't be told until we're ready to leave Jackson Hole.''

"I expect they'll go up into Yellowstone," the colonel said. "Senator Vest is a sponsor of the park there, and that's the only reason I can see for his being along. You have any ideas on when it'll be best to make your move?''

"That's up to you," Slocum said. "Not till we're across the mountains, anyway. But I can't move unless I know when and where you're set to take over.''

"We don't want to wait till they're up in Yellowstone," Williams said. "That's very rough country. Not enough opportunity to manuever. I'm told Jackson Hole is open ground surrounded by mountains, where we can get in and out. I think it should be done in Jackson Hole.''

"Slocum?'' the colonel said.

"We'll be traveling separate again till we cross the divide. Likely it'll take two or three days for us to join up. I figure I'd need a couple of days after that to see how the camp is set up, what the routine is, what the best way is to get to the President. There's plenty of time. Likely we'll make camp in several places. You're going to have to scout that country and decide where the best place is from your point of view. That means another rendezvous after we get into the Hole."

"That's no problem," the colonel said. "That's fine. I have to talk this over with my people and, as you say, we'll have to do some scouting of the country. Once we've decided on the way we want things to go, I'll have Captain Williams here make contact with you. We'll know where you are."

"Fine with me," Slocum said.

"There's one other thing." The colonel was leaning back in his chair, watching Slocum's face; he drew on his cigar and blew a smoke ring toward the ceiling. "You've got only one man with you. Bellows, I believe his name is. Counting the mule skinners, there are more than a hundred men in the President's party. I was expecting you to put together a sufficient force to do this thing properly."

"Two of us is the way to do it proper," Slocum said. "We're not going to overpower the whole of Troop G. We're going to get next to one man and slip him out of camp."

"You have a plan, then."

"Not one I want to talk about yet."

The colonel smiled. "Fair enough. I believe in delegating authority." He stood up, in a way that let

Slocum know he was being dismissed. "I picked you for the job. It's up to you to do the job. It's up to you to do it right. I don't have to tell you the consequences if it's not done right."

The captain saw Slocum out, but he didn't accompany him past the door. Slocum retrieved his bay and headed off along the back of officers' row, thinking about the colonel and that smile of his. The colonel was just a little too happy with himself to be pleasant company, a little too full of his importance and his power. That pleased smile told Slocum he had just been tested, that the question about Bellows had been only a way of seeing if he knew what he was doing, if he would stand up for himself or cave under pressure. Slocum didn't like being put in a position like that. It was of a piece with those two men coming into the stable after him. The colonel had a way of making a man realize he was being used by somebody with the power to make him or break him.

Well, another week or two and he would be rid of the colonel. And that would be the last time he would get himself tied up with politics.

He had just reached the northern fringe of the fort when he met up with the crowd streaming back from the sham battle they'd been watching out on the plain. He had to get the bay up against a building front to let them pass. Wagons and riders and even a buggy or two were struggling along through a mass of soldiers on foot, half of them drunk and the rest of them getting there. He wondered which of the officers trotting past in wagons with their wives was the one the colonel had borrowed the cottage from.

He found Bellows and the women near the back of the crowd. Bellows was taking it easy on the mules, letting the mob get ahead of him. Laura Ryan was on the seat beside him, and the girls were still flushed and bright-eyed from all the excitement.

Slocum fell into line and brought the bay up alongside the near wheeler. "Everybody enjoy the show?"

He got a chorus of assent from the girls. "My ears are still ringing," Gloria said. "Just like a Wild West show, only real. It was thrilling."

"Not very real," Slocum said, "but a hell of a lot realer than anything Bill Cody'll show you. Hope nobody got killed."

Bellows grinned. "A lot of troopers would have bit the dust for sure, if they hadn't been using blanks. Those Indians had 'em outnumbered about five to one." Gloria was clinging to his shoulder, and he looked a little flushed himself; he wasn't used to playing the exotic frontiersman to a bunch of pretty girls, all of them hanging on his every word. "You weren't gone very long," he said. "You see your friend?"

"I saw him," Slocum said. "Tell you about it later. Right now let's get out of this crowd. Put those mules to a trot and let's get back to camp."

9

Supper that night was a stew Bellows had cooked up in the iron pot. The women weren't too handy at fixing meals in uncivilized conditions like this, and Bellows had been doing the cooking ever since they'd left Green River. The tents were set up so as to be shielded by a grove of willows, but they'd built the campfire down along the bank, where they could see the river. Slocum was still brooding about the colonel, and he was content to eat in silence, watching the firelight flicker across the faces of the women as they listened spellbound to Bellows's stories. He could see Bellows was enjoying himself; he wasn't likely to get an audience like this again, and he was taking advantage of it.

He was going on now about old Washakie's virtues as a chief. "You got to understand, Washakie ain't even a full-blood Shoshone," he said. "His father was a Flathead, I think, and Washakie didn't even start living amongst the Shoshone till he was in his twenties, after a Crow raid made his ma a widow and sent her back to her tribe.

"Now, his ma's an interesting story. A friend of mine, a fella named Nick Wilson, got himself adopted by Washakie's ma when he was a boy. Nick was one of the original Pony Express riders. I think he's driving an overland stage somewhere now, but he was an army scout when I met him. But this happened back in 'fifty-four or 'fifty-five, down around Great Salt Lake. Indians moved around a lot in those days. Anyway, Washakie's old ma, she'd lost a husband killed by Crows, two sons in a snowslide and a daughter dragged to death by a horse, and she got to grieving so bad couldn't anybody do anything with her. Then she had a dream. Dreamt a white boy would come to be her son. Got so it was a real fixation with her.

"Nick was about eleven then, put out by his family to herd sheep, and he'd learned to talk Indian from a Gosiute boy working the sheep with him. Shoshone and Gosiute, they're something alike, and when some of the braves heard about this Indian-talking boy, they figured he was just what Washakie's ma needed. Went to Washakie and offered to steal Nick away from his family. Washakie, though, being a friend of whites, wouldn't hear of it. But he said it'd be all right if they could get Nick to come live with 'em on his own hook."

The women were listening with rapt attention. Only the trickle of the river off in the dark could be heard as Bellows spoke. "And did he?" Laura Ryan asked. "Did he go voluntarily?"

"Yes, ma'am. Said he was tired of herding sheep. Indians offered him a pinto pony of his own and said all he'd have to do was hunt and fish and ride horses every day. Nick said that sounded fine to him, and he snuck off one night to meet up with the tribe and went off with them. Lived with them for two years. Washakie's ma, she took to him right off, loved him like a real son, and Washakie, he treated him just like a brother. He had a fine time." Bellows laughed. "Told me once he was out hunting elk with Washakie and some braves when his horse ran off on him and he got lost. Night coming on, he got to worrying about bears, and he climbed himself a tree. The Indians was hunting him, of course, and when they finally found him, they wanted to know what he was doing up that tree. Well, Nick, he didn't want to admit he was scared, so he told 'em he was looking for his horse. And one of the braves, he sorta suggested Nick climb down. Kindly-like, you know. Said, wherever his horse was, he wouldn't find it up there."

When the laughter had subsided, Gloria asked, "Why did he live with them for only two years, if he was so happy with them?"

"Well, word came that his father was getting up an armed party to capture him. Nick didn't believe it, and neither did Washakie, and it turned out not to be true, but that was one time Washakie found himself outvoted. The tribe decided that Nick had to go home. So Washakie's wife and his ma, they fixed Nick up in his best buckskins and sent him home to his family."

"It must have broken her heart," Mrs. Ryan said. "His Shoshone mother."

"That's just what it did," Bellows said. "See, Nick was planning on going right back. But his pa died just after he got home, and he had to help support the family. Then along about eighteen-and-sixty he went off to join the Pony Express. Near got his scalp lifted, too, and he still won't take his hat off, even indoors, on account of a scar where he took an arrow over one eye.

"But what I'm getting at is the end of the story. Him leaving just broke his old Indian ma's heart, like you said. Got so she'd go off for days and nobody could find her. And while Nick was off with the Pony Express, she set out to find him. This was six or seven years after he'd left the tribe. The tribe had moved on, and even Nick's family had moved, but she found 'em, God knows how, still down around Great Salt Lake. And she lived there with Nick's real ma for two months, waiting for him to come home.

"It's said they got real close, the two women, though couldn't either of them speak a word the other knew. Nick got home after his Indian ma had give up and gone off, and his real ma told him he had to go find her. See, they'd got that close. Maybe both of 'em being widows gave 'em something in common. That and Nick. Anyway, Nick caught up with Washakie and the tribe around South Pass, not too far from here—which'll give you an idea of how far she'd traveled to find him—but she'd died by the time he got there."

The end of the story brought a silence around the fire, the women likely thinking of that old Indian woman grieving for her departed white son, but Bellows didn't let them dwell on it. He launched into other stories about Washakie—how he'd been close friends with men like Jim Bridger and Kit Carson; how he'd pressed the government for a reservation for his tribe until in 1868 they deeded him the land he wanted, 4,297 square miles of this rich hunting ground; and how he'd gone over the reservation treaty with two interpreters and a fine-tooth comb till he was sure it contained everything he'd asked for: a school and teachers, a church and a mill, a hospital, seed and farm tools, and the permanent posting of an army garrison to ward off his Indian enemies.

The women were starry-eyed by the time they drifted sleepily off to their tents and Slocum finally got around to telling Bellows about his meeting with the colonel.

"So he didn't like it that there's only two of us," Bellows said. "Likely it hurts his sense of economy to think of fifty thousand dollars split only two ways."

"I hope it hurts him somewhere," Slocum said. "I don't trust our friend the colonel—whatever his name is. In a deal like this, men playing high politics, everybody's got to watch his own back."

"I been watching my back since I was grown," Bellows said. "So have you. It's nothing new. Just keep thinking about that money."

Slocum stayed at the fire after Bellows had wandered up through the willows to his tent. The fire was dying, and there was a chill in the air; even in August the nights got cold in this country. After a while he heard stifled giggles from the direction of the tent and figured Bellows had Gloria in there with him. He knew Laura Ryan was waiting for him in hers, but he wanted to be alone a while yet, out here by the fire in the night with the black sky overhead and the river murmuring quietly off in the dark.

He wasn't used to spending this much time in such close quarters with so many people. Having the women along spoiled his concentration, and he knew he was going to need every bit of concentration he had to set this thing up and pull it off without getting caught or killed. It amounted to the same thing, because if they caught him, they would surely hang him.

He wondered what would happen to Laura Ryan if they got caught and the colonel's side lost and there was no one to protect her. He seemed to remember there was a woman in that plot to kill Lincoln so many years ago, and that they'd hanged the woman the same as they had the men. He didn't like the picture that gave him: Laura Ryan with her neck twisted, her face blue, and her tongue sticking out. He didn't like the picture of himself that way, either.

That made him think of Arthur. What would happen if it turned out he was guilty of what they claimed? Would they hang the President of the United States? They'd been known to chop the head off a king or two back on the other side of the Atlantic, and if they got a confession out of Arthur, they'd probably have no choice but to hang him. Likely the country would demand it; for sure, the newspapers would be calling for his head. And the man would deserve it too. But it made Slocum glad he hadn't met him up close; it was easier to turn a man over to a thing like that if you didn't know him well. And he didn't intend on getting to know him well, either. Just work out the plan, snatch him, and turn him over. Let the colonel and his people take it from there.

He decided Bellows was right. All this thinking was doing him no good at all. The thing to think on was the money—and Laura Ryan. Laura had ways of making a man stop thinking when his mind began to run away with him.

He tossed the last of his coffee into the fire,

causing a sudden hiss of steam, and stood up to kick the remainder of it out. When he was sure the coals were dead, he dropped the cup in the water bucket they used for washing dishes and headed up into the willows.

Lanterns still glowed in all the tents. He heard sounds in Bellows's tent as he passed, but he couldn't see anything. They'd draped rawhide curtains along the inside walls like the Indians did to prevent those shadowy silhouettes a lantern usually threw against the canvas.

Laura Ryan was lying awake in the buffalo-robe pallet when he ducked in through the tent flap. The army had supplied a folding cot, but there was no way two people could fit on it. And with willow branches laid right under the buffalo robe, the pallet was as comfortable as many a bed he'd slept on. She had the Sibley stove going, the stovepipe running up through the insulated vent in the canvas roof.

She smiled when she saw him. "I thought you'd never come to bed."

He kicked off his boots and started shucking his clothes. "I got to thinking out there by the fire. Fires do that to me sometimes. Out under a big sky with nothing but the night all around."

"I like it," she said. "The country's beautiful. I wouldn't want to live out here, and I don't think I'd like it if I were alone, but I can see how people get attached to it. What was it you were thinking about?"

"Night thoughts."

"Good or bad?"

"Not good. I don't much like this job I'm doing."

She smiled again. "This job? Shepherding a bunch of women through the wilderness?"

"No—the job that this one's a cover for."

"Don't think about it. I assume you're being paid a lot of money. Think about the money."

"That's what Clay says: think about the money. Used to be I could do that, and that was enough. Maybe I'm getting old. There's some things I don't want to do any more. Even for a lot of money."

"Then think about this," she said, and peeled the buffalo robe down to open up the pallet.

She was lying there stark naked, long and pink and voluptuous in the lantern light, her red hair spilled out around her head. Watching his eyes, she ran her hands up her ribcage to palm those large, big-nippled breasts, her knees coming up and sagging apart. He felt that old spasm of excitement suddenly seize his innards, and he took off the rest of his clothes, already erect by the time he was as naked as she was.

"Come to bed," she said. "No, leave the lantern lit. I like to be able to see. Just come to bed."

Grateful that he had her to drown himself in, he slipped into the buffalo robe, in between her legs, and into her. Slowly they began to move together, and soon he had no thoughts at all.

10

Traveling by a separate route, they didn't join up with the Presidential party till it was over the divide and starting down the Gros Ventre River.

Crossing the Wind River range was rough going. Bellows knew the lay of the land and without too much trouble found a mountain pass they could negotiate with the wagons, but felling trees to cut trail held them to a pretty slow pace, and several times they had to ask the women to get out and walk as the mules struggled up a particularly steep stretch of ground. Coming down was in some ways worse than the uphill trek had been; for most of the way, they just lashed the wheel spokes to the axles and locked the brakes in place, creating a drag that kept the wagons from overrunning the mules. Despite some occasional grousing about the discomforts of overland travel, the women kept their spirit of adventure; they were still a little in awe of where they found themselves, overcome by the scenery, and delighted by the sight of deer and moose and the occasional herd of elk they flushed out of the woods ahead of them. Only once did they get spooked, when a bear came sniffing around camp in the dead of night. Slocum and Bellows had to promise to stand watch till dawn, and even so it was two or three hours before the women finally settled down enough to get back to sleep.

They caught up with the Arthur party at its first encampment on the Gros Ventre. The terrain had leveled out some, and the party of women escorted by Slocum and Bellows had had a fairly easy day, crossing a final ridge and coming down out of the woods in the early evening to see what looked to be half a hundred campfires dotting the south bank of the river. Wood smoke drifted in the air, and from somewhere beyond the tents scattered through the trees came the raucous honking of the pack train's mules. As they cleared the bottom of the ridge, still several hundred yards from the campsite, Slocum began to see blue-uniformed troopers around many of the fires, and somewhere some old soldier was playing "The Battle Hymn of the Republic" on a mouth harp. It wasn't Slocum's army, and it wasn't his song, but it gave him a sudden sharp memory of other campsites, with soldiers in Confederate gray sitting around fires in the dusk, playing or singing that other anthem, the call to fight for Dixie, against men in the same Union blue worn by these men here. He couldn't see any pickets out, but the men charged with protecting their President might be a little touchy about strangers approaching out of the twilight, so he halted the wagons a good two hundred yards from the first of the tents and sent Bellows on ahead to bring back Lieutenant Troy.

Troy was short and thickset, a little old for a lieutenant—Slocum figured he'd probably held a higher brevet rank at one time—and he had a way of being officious. Likely he found his present job demeaning, but in the presence of Mrs. Ryan he was polite, at least.

"You can settle here," he told them. "My orders are that you're to camp at least two hundred yards back of the main party, wherever we are. Your site'll be off limits to everybody but me, and I'll be disturbing you only when carrying out my job makes it necessary."

"I see no sense in that," Slocum said. "Separating us on the way out made sense, when the newspapers might have got wind of it, but you can't keep us secret now. By dawn every man in camp will know we're here."

"All I know is what my orders are," Troy said. "The whole area between you and the main camp's off limits. You'll have privacy, anyway. We'll put a couple of sentries at the edge of the main camp to keep anybody from wandering back here."

Their arrival must have been eagerly awaited; Troy said that all four of the girls had been requested for that night. Slocum and Bellows began unloading the wagons and setting up camp, but the girls barely had time to down a quick supper and freshen up a bit when Troy returned to escort the first of them to the tent of whichever of Arthur's bunch had asked for her. These dealings were worked out between Troy and Mrs. Ryan. Slocum had no part in them, but from what Mrs. Ryan told him, that would be the pattern for the entire trip. Troy would be told which man wanted a woman and when—and which woman if a man grew to prefer a particular one—and Troy himself would come to escort her to the man's tent, lingering at a discreet distance till she emerged so he could escort her back again. Maybe it was just a matter of sneaking a defenseless girl past a hundred womanless men, but the attempt at secrecy still struck Slocum as absurd.

"I guess they got to keep up appearances," he told Bellows. "That's the way that kind of mind works. Long as they pretend we're not here, we don't exist, officially."

The party worked its way slowly down the Gros Ventre, staying each place only so long as the President found the fishing to his taste, then striking camp and moving on to the next location. With their skills as guides no longer needed, Slocum and Bellows found themselves reduced to menial chores: chopping wood for the campfires and the Sibley stoves, digging pits for garbage, taking down and putting up tents, and building a makeshift canvas-sided privy for every new encampment. Slocum had a lot of spare time, and he spent it scouting the layout of the main camp, checking on where the sentires were, and trying to get a fix on how best to get to Arthur. Arthur and his entourage spent every day fishing from the riverbank, and now a lot of the mule skinners were trying their luck at it too, but Slocum stayed as far away from the President as he could.

Each campsite was laid out more or less like the last, following the line of the river, with the women's camp two hundred yards to the rear and sentries at the off-limits line. The first tents beyond the off-limits line were those of the mule skinners, and the cavalry escort was bivouacked beyond that, just short of a large area roped off for their mounts and the pack animals. The tents allotted to Arthur and his friends were set off somewhat from the rest; a big plot was reserved for Arthur himself, with enough ground around his tent to give him total privacy. The perimeter of the plot was constantly patrolled by sentries. Slocum figured getting to him would be possible, but it wouldn't be easy. A bar tent had been set up more or less in the middle of the main camp, where the liquor was free for the asking, and most of the mule skinners and some of the cavalry escort spent their nights getting drunk in there. Slocum stayed away from it; he didn't want his face getting too well known in this crowd.

They came out of the Gros Ventre River canyon early on a sunny afternoon and set up camp again on the southeast bank of the Gros Ventre just where it spilled into the Snake. The Snake was fairly wide here, fast and clear, running south through the valley that was Jackson Hole.

Slocum had never been in the Hole before, and it was almost as much of an experience for him as it was for the women. It was a high mountain valley, green and grassy and flat as a wood floor, ringed with peaks, and with little marshy creeks meandering through stands of cottonwoods and white-barked aspen. Deer and elk were plentiful, and even moose were a common sight, and the sky overhead was clear and blue in the thin air. The Tetons rose almost straight up along the entire western rim of the valley. The little suggestion of foothills didn't mar that impression: great, rocky snow peaks rising almost vertically eight thousand feet above the valley floor.

"Quite a place," he said to Bellows.

"Always looked like the Happy Hunting Ground to me," Bellows said, "but the Indians never hunted here much. Not enough buffalo up here, and what's a hunt without buffalo?''

A small band of Arapaho had their lodges set up across the Snake from where they'd made camp, and a cavalry squad crossed the river to make their acquaintance through one of the Indian scouts guiding the main party. The Arapaho, a sub-band of the tribe sharing Washakie's reservation, were delighted to find themselves in the presence of the Great White Father from beyond where the sun rose and immediately proposed a celebration in his honor—a tribal dance to be held that afternoon.

The women wanted to see the show, but the protocol laid down by Troy wouldn't allow them into the main camp except at night, when they were there to ply their trade, so Slocum had to tell them no.

''Might shock some of them young troopers, seeing the women their President's brought along for his recreation,'' he said. ''You stick close to your tents. We'll tell you all about it when we get back.''

The rhythmic beat of Indian drums was throbbing in the air by the time Slocum and Bellows left the tent area, riding up through the trees along the riverbank toward the main camp. Except for two sentries at the off-limits line, the camp itself was deserted; everybody had headed for that broad, round point of land at the mouth of the Gros Ventre, where the show was already underway. The Indians had left their lodges and crossed the Snake. Slocum could see feathered heads bobbing in ritual dance above the crowd behind the row of camp chairs set up for Arthur and his entourage. He and Bellows worked their horses around through the trees to the right of the crowd, where they had a clear view.

The Arapaho seemed to have worked themselves to a pretty high pitch already. About fifteen braves were bending and stomping and rearing in a tight circle, stripped to breechclouts and moccasins, the bells strapped around their ankles jingling in time with the drums. They wore full war paint and were shaking rattles and coupsticks and tomahawks, singing a hoarse-voiced chant that rose and fell with the rhythmic beat of the drums. The whole band had come across; the squaws were hunkered down along the bank of the Snake, kids and camp dogs and all. The dancers were between them and the crowd of onlookers. The drummers were down near the other end of the crowd, three or four Indians crouched around each of three big bowl-shaped drums stretched taut with rawhide, the drummers wielding sticks in both hands. The drummers looked a little less war-like than the dancers; most of them wore white men's shirts, and two or three had floppy hats on their heads, but they, too, were singing.

"I'm not sure it's a good idea letting 'em see the Great White Father's a mere mortal," Bellows said. "Maybe they're tame, but they ain't been tame long, and you can bet them braves have tasted blood in battle. One of 'em just might decide to count himself a very big coup. Killing the chief of all the white men would be about the biggest coup there is."

Slocum saw Arthur in the middle of the row of chairs, leaning forward, watching intently. General Sheridan was next to him, affecting less interest, leaning back with his legs crossed and a pipe in his mouth, but the others in the row seemed as fascinated as Arthur, trying to take everything in at once. Slocum identified the old man the colonel had said was Senator Vest of Missouri, and he thought he recognized old Abe Lincoln's son, Robert, Arthur's Secretary of War. Good thing this was just a ritual ceremony; one fast jump and those Arapaho could wipe out a good part of the whole U. S. government.

"I wonder if it's occurred to anybody that this is what the Indians do to work themselves up before battle," he said. "They've got themselves into a pretty good frenzy already. You think maybe they been at some firewater?"

"Good Indian don't need firewater to get himself into a frenzy," Bellows said. "That dancing'll do it. That stomping and circling, the jingling and all that drumming and chanting will make an Indian drunk as any firewater."

The dancers did seem to be working themselves into some kind of trance. They were shuffling and stomping in a tight circle, bending forward almost to the ground, then rearing up and throwing their heads back, eyes closed, sweat running down their bodies, rattles shaking, and drums keeping time with that hoarse-voiced chant. The chant was almost hypnotic itself, a rising and falling *HAU-hau-hau-hau, HAU-hau-hau-hau, HAU-hau-hau-hau* that had even the squaws' heads bobbing in time. Slocum watched one of the braves start to shuffle out away from the rest, jigging around in a tight little circle of his own, twirling his tomahawk over his head. His head was thrown back, his eyes clenched tight, his voice keeping up that hoarse chant. The men in the chairs started shrinking back as the circle brought him around toward them, but Arthur seemed to lean even farther forward, watching with fascination.

The brave's eyes popped suddenly open then, feverish and wild, and he whooped above the chant and leaped toward Arthur.

Slocum had the spurs sunk into the bay before he even realized it, and he lunged forward, his Colt out. White men were spilling out of the chairs, but Arthur seemed frozen to his, open-mouthed. The bay hit the brave with barely a yard to spare, knocking him sideways, but his frenzy kept him on his feet, spinning back along the bay's side, that tomahawk still twirling above his head. Slocum drove a boot into his side and brought his Colt around in a vicious swipe that he could feel shatter the man's wrist, knocking the tomahawk to the ground. And then the bay's lunge carried him past, and he wheeled it around to see that the man had gone down. The other braves were leaping to grab him, troopers jumping over the chairs to join in the melee, beating the renegade to the ground with fists and pistol butts and boots until he was buried under a wriggling pile of buckskin and blue.

The drums had stopped; squaws were shrieking, snatching up their kids and running for the River. Slocum could see what was left of the band waving their arms and jabbering at the crowd, likely hoping to forestall an attack on themselves. Arthur had dropped back into his chair, white-faced, but Sheridan was on his feet, his pistol out. Slocum saw him glance from the Indians to the troopers, and saw a quick decision made as Sheridan waved back troopers drawing their guns and leaped to start pulling men off the renegade.

Men were running past Slocum to get at the pile, but so far nobody was paying him any mind. That wouldn't last long; as soon as things were under control, he figured he'd find himself the center of attention, and that was the last thing he wanted. He wheeled the bay and sent it at a trot through the crowd to meet up with Bellows, who was circling his paint around the back of the chairs.

"I'll vow you just won yourself a medal," Bellows said, watching the melee out front. "Told you this wasn't a good idea."

"I don't want a medal," Slocum said. "If I could think as fast as I move, I'd have let somebody else handle that. Under the circumstances, I'd just as soon not stand out in this crowd."

Sheridan and the other officers were pulling the pile of men apart. The renegade brave was wrestled to his feet, two other Arapaho holding his arms behind his back, others crowding around gesticulating and jabbering. One of them struck the renegade in the face with the flat of his hand and went on jabbering at Sheridan, whipping the same hand across his own throat as if to make his point clear.

"What do you think they'll do with him?" Slocum said.

"Anybody's guess," Bellows said. "For sure it wasn't planned. They wouldn't have brought their women over here if it was. And they ain't so crazy as to plan something like that in front of a whole troop of cavalry. What we got is one self-intoxicated brave, but if he'd reached his target we'd have had a real little massacre. There'd be slaughtered Arapaho all over that riverbank."

"Let's get away from here," Slocum said. "Somebody's going to want to know who we are, and I'd just as soon avoid that, if we can.''

They headed back through the camp at a trot. Troopers were running for the tents and bringing out their carbines, not sure yet just what they were faced with, but Slocum figured Sheridan had things under control. One of the sentries shouted a question at them as they crossed the off-limits line, but Slocum ignored it, wanting to get back to the tent area before anybody figured out who had stopped that brave. He could still hear shouting behind him as they neared the tents, and the women were all up on their feet and looking his way.

They came running out to meet them as he and Bellows reined up beside the first tent. ''What's happened?'' Laura Ryan said. ''The drums stopped so quickly, and then there was all that shouting and people running. Is something wrong?''

''Came close,'' Slocum said, ''but it's all right. Nothing to worry about.''

''Renegade brave got himself all worked up,'' Bellows said. ''Tried to lift the President's scalp. Would have too but Slocum here stopped him.''

Mrs. Ryan clapped her hands to her mouth, and there was a collective gasp from the other women.

''Did the President get hurt?'' Gloria asked.

''No, but I think Slocum broke that brave's arm. About fifty people piled on him and wrestled him down. He's lucky somebody didn't shoot him. They may shoot him yet.''

Slocum swung down off the bay and began to unloosen the saddle cinch. ''Somebody fetch me a bottle. I need a drink.''

Things up at the main camp seemed to have quieted down some by the time he got the bay unsaddled. Gloria had fetched him a bottle and a glass, and he was working on his second drink when he heard a horse approaching from the direction of the off-limits line and looked up to see Lieutenant Troy coming through the trees at a trot. He had been afraid of that. He knew Troy wasn't just coming on his usual business of reporting which girls were wanted in which tents tonight.

Troy reined up in front of the tent, but he didn't dismount. "Where'd you go, man? You just saved the President's life. Everybody back there wants to get a look at you."

"Tell 'em I don't want 'em looking," Slocum said. "What are they doing with that renegade Indian?"

"There's been some argument about that. I believe General Sheridan wanted him shot. There was a lot of parleying through an interpreter, though, and I think they've agreed to turn him over to the elders of his band and to punish him according to their own tribal laws. The President knows the entire band's not at fault. He thinks it best if the renegade's own people deal with him. It's you he wants to talk to. He wants to thank you personally."

"Tell him I don't want any thanks."

"Why, man, you have to put in an appearance. Nobody refuses the President. The President wishes to see you, and the President's wish is an order. You can't refuse it. I have orders to bring you."

Wearily, Slocum got to his feet and handed the bottle and glass to Bellows. "Don't drink all that up. I'm going to need it when I get back."

Troy waited while he resaddled the bay. Then

they set off back toward the main camp. Slocum knew this was going to give too many men too good a look at his face, but there was nothing he could do about it. He saw the sentries glancing at him and trading remarks as they crossed the off-limits line. Then men started drifting from their tents to watch as they passed through the camp. Things seemed almost back to normal. The chairs had been removed from the dancing ground, and the officers had put most of the men to work at some detail or other, likely to keep their tempers under control. As they neared the Snake, he could see the Indians across the river already bringing their teepees down, the women rigging up travois poles behind the ponies. There was a lot of jabbering and shouting going on over there. They were obviously intent on getting away before the white-eyes changed their minds and decided to massacre the whole lot of them. It wouldn't have been the first time an Indian camp had been massacred, down to the last woman and child.

Troy angled left and led him toward the bar tent, just around the butt of the little ridge that paralleled the Gros Ventre on its way toward the Snake. The camp chairs had been moved to the front of the tent, and Slocum saw Arthur in a crowd of officers standing around the chairs. The tent itself looked to have been cleared of all the skinners who spent their afternoons there so this meeting could be held in appropriate privacy. Sheridan was talking animatedly with Arthur, and Slocum wondered if he were still trying to convince the President to have that renegade shot. From what he'd heard of Sheridan, that would be just his style.

Troy called a halt about thirty yards from the tent.

They tethered the horses to a tree, and Slocum followed Troy over to the row of chairs. Arthur came forward to meet him, his hand already outstretched.

"Glad you could come," the President said. As if he'd had any choice, Slocum thought. "Lieutenant Troy, thank you. Mr. Slocum, please have a drink with me and my friends. I want to express my heartfelt thanks for your action. If it hadn't been for your quick thinking, I might not be standing here."

Slocum allowed his hand to be shaken. "I'd have done the same for any man. I did it without thinking, really."

"The point is, you did it," Arthur said. "I have the hair on my head to prove it. I'm grateful there was a man of your experience near enough to react in time. Come and meet the rest of these men."

The others stepped forward one at a time to shake hands as Arthur introduced them: General Sheridan, Senator Vest, Secretary of War Lincoln, and a couple of other civilians Slocum hadn't heard of and whose names he didn't catch. Last to be introduced were two lieutenant-colonels, a man named Gregory and Lieutenant-Colonel Sheridan, the general's nephew. "Colonels Gregory and Sheridan have been assigned to keep a day-to-day log of our trip," Arthur said. "I'll see that your deed is prominently mentioned, Mr. Slocum."

Slocum would just as soon the deed weren't mentioned anywhere, at least not with his name attached to it, but he politely shook all the hands. He had a little trouble concealing his distaste when he found himself face to face with General Sheridan. He remembered Sheridan too well from the war, even after twenty years. It was Sheridan who had laid waste to the valley of the Shenandoah, causing havoc not even Sherman's march to the sea could surpass. And what left the bad taste in a man's mouth was the evident pleasure with which Sheridan had viewed his handiwork. Even now Slocum could remember what Sheridan had reported proudly at the time: that the Shenandoah was so devastated that a crow flying over it would have to carry its own rations.

Arthur showed everybody to a seat and called for drinks. He seated Slocum on his left, General Sheridan on his right, and the rest in a little semicircle. Slocum didn't like the feeling of being on display; now he could see even mule skinners and troopers wandering up through the trees for a closer look.

The drinks were served by a young lieutenant, evidently somebody's aide. When everybody had a glass, General Sheridan proposed a toast to Slocum. Slocum almost drank before he remembered a man didn't drink a toast to himself in civilized society.

"Needless to say," Arthur said, "I'm happy you're a member of our party. I hope you've found everything suitable. No problems?"

"Everything's suitable, " Slocum said. "I've had no problems."

While Arthur talked on, Slocum found himself examining Robert Lincoln, who was sitting in the last chair on the left. If there was one man here who interested him more than Arthur, it was Lincoln, if only because of whose son he was. Old Abe in many ways had been the principal force in the shaping of Slocum's youth, and maybe his manhood too, if you credited Abraham Lincoln with winning the war. Robert Lincoln didn't look much like his father, but still it was like being in the presence of a legend, even more than sitting next to Arthur was.

The man wasn't as tall as his father, and he had a lot more flesh on his bones, with none of Abe's gauntness, but there was a certain quiet solidity there that was maybe something akin to what you saw in his father's pictures. He was blue-eyed and pale-skinned, and he wore a beard, but it was a full beard complete with moustache, nothing like the famous chin whiskers of his father. He was not a man Slocum would have picked out of a crowd if he hadn't known who his father had been. Just another prosperous-looking gent in a suit and vest. But he seemed straight enough—a man who met your eye when you looked at him.

Arthur seemed a little at a loss as to how to keep the conversation going. Likely he wasn't used to talking with people who were not of his own type. He was going on now about the country they'd passed through, and the kind of life a man must lead out here, and how pleased he was he'd made the trip. "This is magnificent country," he said. "The fishing's been superb, and the game is very impressive. I suppose you take this country for granted, Mr. Slocum, but there's nothing like this east of the Mississippi."

"It's good country, all right," Slocum said. "Getting a little crowded the past few years, but good country. I've never been up here in Jackson Hole before, but I've been near everywhere else. Been west of the Mississippi for close to twenty years."

He'd been watching Arthur closely, trying to get a hold on how he felt about this man he would soon be snatching out of this camp if the colonel ever showed.

The President of the country: somehow it didn't seem real. He was just another portly man in a business suit, a man with wavy hair and black eyes, his muttonchops gray and descending all the way down the line of his jaw. The only thing out of the ordinary was the strange little brimless cap on his head and the leather leggings laced up over his boots to his knees.

Slocum became aware of General Sheridan's eyes on him. "Do I hear a hint of the South in your voice, Mr. Slocum?" Sheridan asked. "Georgia, maybe?"

"Good guess," Slocum said. "I was born and raised in Georgia—Calhoun County."

"How is it a man from Georgia finds himself out here?"

"Well, General, you might say you had a little to do with it. You and Mr. Lincoln's father, President Lincoln. That, and a carpetbagger who took a fancy to the land my family owned."

"You were in the War, then. Fighting for the Confederacy, I take it."

"Yes, and I'm proud of it. But I came west in 'sixty-five, and put the States behind me."

The general smiled and raised his eyebrows. He evidently thought he was making a friendly joke. "I hope we didn't meet on a battlefield somewhere," he said.

"Couldn't say," Slocum said. "Don't know all the battlefields you were on. Half the time, I didn't know what battlefield *I* was on. People can look it all up now, with maps and names and dates, but to us it was just mud and dust and thirst and blood. But I don't look back. What's past is past."

"A wise way of thinking," Arthur said, obviously looking for a way to change the subject. "Let me drink to your success, Mr. Slocum. We need men like you to settle this part of the country. All this will be brought into the United States because of men like you, and someday the nation will stretch from the Atlantic to the Pacific. What's your part of our expedition? How have we employed you?"

Slocum glanced toward Lieutenant Troy, who was lingering behind the row of chairs with a group of his fellow officers. "Not sure I should say," he said.

"I beg your pardon?" Arthur asked.

"I'm not part of the main bunch. I'm with the Chicago contingent."

"Chicago contingent?"

Slocum saw one of the officers behind the chairs bend to whisper something in Arthur's ear. Arthur listened and nodded, and Slocum saw something change in his face, a flash of embarrassment which he quickly covered over. "I see," he said, and seemed in a hurry to change the subject again. "You seem a very competent man. The very picture we Easterners conjure up when we imagine the West. The way you're dressed—I suppose that's the garb of a cowboy. Is that your usual occupation?"

Slocum smiled. "I wouldn't call them cowboys, Mr. President. Cowhands, maybe. Most of them may be young, but they ain't boys. I've been a cowhand, bounty hunter—been a lot of things. But it ain't considered polite out here to inquire too close into a man's past."

"Ah," Arthur said, "I see." He seemed to be fumbling for some way to bring the interview to an end. "Well, I hope we have the benefit of your experience on the rest of the trip. We'll be going up into the Yellowstone country next. Senator Vest is determined that I'm to see Yellowstone, and I understand it's worth seeing. I'm pleased that we have you along. But I said that, didn't I? General Sheridan, can we get Mr. Slocum another drink?"

"Thanks," Slocum said, "but one drink's plenty. I got to be getting back. There's chores to do. But I thank you just the same. It's been an honor meeting you gentlemen. Now, if you'll excuse me, I'll be taking my leave."

Invitations to stay came from all along the line of chairs, but Slocum could tell they were all happy to see him go. Maybe some had overheard what his job was here, or maybe this idea of sitting around making small talk with a hired hand wasn't one they'd fancied from the start. He wanted to get away himself; it wasn't pleasant chatting over a drink with the man you were being paid to betray. Especially a man whose life you'd just saved—a man who was the President of your country.

The men all rose to shake his hand again, and Arthur accompanied him a short way back toward his horse. "I just want to thank you once again," he said. "I'm very grateful to you. And I'm grateful for the job you're doing here. Every part of our expedition needs guides, and I understand you were chiefly hired as a guide. I apologize for that little awkwardness. If I'd known, I'd never have asked the question." His face broke out in what seemed a genuinely friendly smile. "Maybe if I'm out here a little longer. I'll learn the Western custom of not inquiring too much into a man's business. I hope to see you

again before the journey's over. If you need anything at all, just convey it through the lieutenant
assigned to your party, and I'll see that it's done.''

Slocum swung up onto the bay and headed back
through the camp, still aware of the troopers and
mule skinners watching him as he passed. He couldn't
help wondering what Arthur's attitude would be if
the man knew the real reason he'd hired on to this
expedition. And he would find out soon enough—as
soon as Colonel Smith made contact and put the
thing in motion. At least Arthur hadn't asked him to
be discreet about the women. He had shown him the
courtesy of taking that for granted. All in all, he
seemed a decent man, not the kind who could be
guilty of what the colonel suggested.

Bellows was sitting out in front of his tent when
Slocum dismounted and started unsaddling the bay.
He still had the bottle, and from the looks of it, he'd
been working at it pretty steadily.

"Where are the women?" Slocum asked.

"Down taking baths in the river," Bellows said.
"You get to meet the Great White Father? He offer
to strike you off a medal?"

"I don't want a medal. All I want is to get this
thing over with. Where the hell's the colonel?"

"Patience, John, patience. That kind of money's
worth a lot of patience. Something got your dander
up?"

"There's just been something spooking me about
this from the start. Gives a man a funny feeling, what
we're fixing to do. Almost like I'd planned to snatch
old Jeff Davis out of his office back during the
War."

"I thought you said you put the States behind you

when you came west. If that's so, Chester Arthur's nothing to you. Not like old Jeff Davis was, anyway.''

"Maybe he shouldn't be, but it feels like it. Especially now I've met him up close, talked with him, had a drink with him. He seems like a decent sort of man.''

"All politicians seem decent. Hell, that's the first skill a man's got to have to go into that business— making folks think he's a decent sort of man. Don't let him fool you.''

Slocum hunkered down beside him and took the bottle. "You know, Clay, sometimes I think you're a mistrustful man.''

"Why, hell, of course I am. I don't trust any man I ain't tested in the fire, and there ain't enough of them worth counting. Give me that bottle back. You sound like you need more than a drink. Why don't you go find Mrs. Ryan. She'll take your mind off things.''

"Thanks,'' Slocum said. "I believe I will.''

11

The next afternoon Slocum and Bellows were up on the little slope south of camp cutting wood. The slope rose up no more than a hundred feet high here, paralleling the Gros Ventre and petering out just short of the bar tent in the middle of the main camp, where Slocum had had his audience with Arthur the day before. From up here Slocum could see the women's tents directly below, the stream of the Gros Ventre behind them, and as far west up the riverbank to where the main camp began just beyond the off-limits line. The rest of camp was blocked from sight by the timber, mostly lodgepole pine here. They'd been working for the better part of an hour, their horses tethered in the trees, when Slocum heard something on the slope above him and looked up to see Captain Williams carefully walking his mount down through the brush.

"Here's our man," he said. "And about time too."

Williams reined to a halt about twenty yards up the hill, scanning the riverbank below. When he had scouted all the ground in sight, he dismounted and led his horse stealthily down the slope. Slocum saw that the horse's hooves were encased in makeshift rawhide stockings, lashed around the fetlock, so it would leave less in the way of tracks.

"I see you found us," he said. "I was beginning to think you and the colonel had got yourselves lost out here."

"We've been tracking you for days," Williams said. He was still watching the riverbank, and he looked a little jumpy, as though perhaps being so near to Arthur and knowing what he was planning was starting to give him the jitters. "You two free to leave? Anybody expecting you anywhere?"

"We're free to do as we please," Bellows said. "Arthur's got his own guides. Nothing for us to do but chop wood and haul water."

"Well, there'll be more for you to do soon enough," Williams said. "The colonel wants to see you." He took an armful of rawhide squares out of his saddlebags, like the ones he had lashed to the hooves of his mount. "Put these on your horses. If any of those sentries spot the tracks, they'll think these are unshod Indian ponies."

"You see any sentries up there?" Slocum said.

"Not on the way down just now, but they're patrolling pretty regular. They're not taking it too serious, just idling along on horseback, a pair at a time, but they make a complete circle all the way around the camp. Hard to tell where you might run into them."

When Slocum and Bellows had the rawhide squares lashed in place, they mounted up and followed Williams back up the slope. He turned east along the spine of the ridge, climbing up through the timber to where it gradually gave way to spruce and fir. Soon they were high enough to see back across the valley to where the Tetons rose up white and craggy against the blue of the sky. They backtracked along the ridge for about a mile, and then Williams cut down across a brushy ravine and led them up another ridge, higher this time, and turned west again. After another two hundred yards, he reined up at the edge of a brushy little draw down off to the left and pointed to the ridge on the other side of it.

"Sentries have been coming up that ridge on their circle," he said, "so keep your eyes open. We got people watching, but we don't want to get caught by surprise."

They followed him down into the draw, picking their way carefully through the brush so as to make as little noise as possible. Coming up the other side, Slocum saw a blue uniform through the blur of the brush. A man was sitting hunkered down against a tree trunk at the crest of the ridge, but it wasn't the colonel; it was a lieutenant, a man Slocum hadn't seen before. He was evidently one of the colonel's bunch, though; he just waved when he caught sight of Williams, and they passed him heading straight uphill into denser timber. About thirty yards up, Williams called a halt and swung down off his mount.

"We'll have to lead the horses from here on," he said. "Gets pretty tight up in there."

Slocum and Bellows dismounted and followed Williams up into a narrow little ravine, barely more than a crevice in the hillside, overgrown with brush and trees. They hadn't gone ten yards when the colonel came in sight, up where the ravine became impassable, his horse tethered alongside another, likely the lieutenant's mount, and he himself leaning back against a tree trunk. They tied their own horses to a tree and climbed the last few feet up to him.

The colonel was back in uniform. He looked as

happy with himself as always, smiling that broad smile, but he didn't rise to greet them. "Good to see you again," he said. "Pick a piece of ground and let's talk. I understand you had a little excitement in camp yesterday."

"A little," Slocum said. "How'd you know about it?"

The colonel tapped the field glasses hanging around his neck on a strap. "We've been keeping you under observation. Couldn't see much from where we were, but there looked to be a lot of commotion after that tom-tom ceremony, and those Indians sure left in a hurry. What was the trouble?"

"Renegade brave tried to lift the President's scalp," Bellows said. "Got himself all worked up and tried to count coup on the Great White Father. Slocum here put him out of action. Saved old Arthur's hide and got himself invited to tea on account of it."

The colonel looked at Slocum, eyebrows raised. "You met the President?"

"Something of a command performance," Slocum said. "We had a drink and a little talk. Him and his cronies. Maybe I should have let that brave alone. Would have saved us all a lot of trouble."

"We want the President alive, Mr. Slocum. He's no use to us dead."

Slocum was glad to hear it. He was beginning to like this job less all the time, even as it was, and he wanted no part of a plan to kill Arthur.

"You got your people out here?" he asked. "I'd like to get this thing over with."

"Let's say we're close enough to be ready when it's done," the colonel said. "What are Arthur's plans? Where are you going when you break camp here?''

''North, up into Yellowstone. We haven't been here long, so I figure we'll be a day or so more. And likely we'll follow the Snake north as far as it's passable. The President likes the fishing.''

The colonel traded glances with Williams. ''That means it'll have to be done here. We've been scouting the country and we've picked out a spot to take him over from you. It's downstream, about twenty miles south of here. It won't make any sense to let him get farther north.'' He brought out a cigar and lit it with a match struck off his thumbnail. ''I want to know how you plan to do it. Could be I've an idea or two that'll help.''

''We'll have to do it at night,'' Slocum said. ''It shouldn't be too difficult. I've been watching the way they arrange things with the women. Arthur's asked for a girl every night since we caught up with him. Maybe he's younger than he looks, or maybe he don't get a chance to cut loose too often back in Washington and don't want anything going to waste, whether he feels up to it or not. In any case, Lieutenant Troy comes to get Arthur's girl every night at the same time, about ten o'clock. He escorts the girl to Arthur's tent, waits a good distance away, then escorts her back through camp to her own tent. They've got Arthur's personal campsite guarded pretty tight, but I think I can get in there when Troy's taking the girl in and out.''

''Where is Arthur's campsite relative to the rest of camp?''

''It's on the south end. The camp's laid out in a

kind of L-shape. We're on the eastern end, back along the Gros Ventre. The main camp runs west away from us, up the bank of the Gros Ventre, and then bends south around the butt end of that little ridge Captain Williams found us on today. Arthur's site is at the very south tip of that bend. They got it roped off all the way around, with sentries patrolling every inch of the perimeter, and the ropes have cowbells on 'em so you'd give yourself away just touching one of them. But the site's big enough to hole up in without anybody seeing you once you get in.''

"Getting in sounds pretty difficult," the colonel said. "How do you plan to do it?"

"Here's the funny part," Slocum said. "They got a thing about these women. Everybody in camp knows they're there, but Sheridan and all of them act like it's a secret, as if none of the troopers know about it. So when it comes time for Arthur to get his woman, Troy relieves the sentry on the stretch where he's going to take her through that rope perimeter. Doesn't want the sentry to witness the transaction, I guess. Only thing is, it takes Troy twenty minutes at least to bring the girl, and that stretch is unguarded for the whole twenty minutes. After he brings her, he takes the sentry's place patrolling the perimeter. Then he leaves it unguarded for another twenty minutes when he escorts her back to her tent.''

The colonel smiled. "Protocol, eh? Got to spare everybody's sensibilities. Enlisted men aren't supposed to see their superiors engaging in such things. And from the lazy way these outriders have been patrolling the country around the camp, they aren't worried about security. It's just routine. Can you get to Arthur and get him out of there in twenty minutes?''

"Won't have to," Slocum said. "I figure to lay up in the trees on the butt end of that ridge, waiting for the lieutenant. When he relieves the sentry and goes for the girl, I'll slip inside the perimeter and hide in the brush. I'll be in there all the time the girl is with Arthur. I'll get to Arthur when she leaves and haul him out through the perimeter while Troy's escorting her back to her tent.''

"That should work," the colonel said. "But then you'll have the rest of those sentries around the perimeter to worry about. You need some sort of diversion to draw them off.''

"Already got one planned," Bellows said. "That's my job. They got a bar tent set up in the middle of camp, and half the camp's in there getting drunk every night. The bar tent's maybe sixty, seventy yards northwest of Arthur's tent, and the pack mules are corralled up maybe sixty yards beyond that, where the Gros Ventre meets the Snake. The right kind of commotion around them mules, and I figure half them drunks'll start shooting at everything they see. Especially after yesterday. That put a real Indian scare into everybody. The hullabaloo ought to be enough to draw them sentries off. And, by the time they figure out there wasn't anything to be shooting at, we'll be long gone.''

"Leaving tracks," the colonel said.

"The way I figure it," Slocum said, "they won't even know Arthur's gone till morning. They won't hear anything but a bunch of drunks shooting at shadows. Won't be any reason for them to check Arthur's tent.''

"Maybe," the colonel said. "You'll still be leaving tracks. And tracks can be followed."

"We'll be leaving tracks no matter what," Bellows said.

"Not necessarily." The colonel cut a sharp glance at Slocum. "You ever go down a fast river in a boat? Or on a raft, say?"

The question took Slocum by surprise. "I can't say I have."

"That's the way I want you to do it," the colonel said. "You'll build a raft—this lodgepole pine's just made for that sort of thing—and one of you'll get Arthur to that raft and bring him down the river. The other—probably you, Bellows, since you've had the most scouting experience—will take the horses and head north, up toward Yellowstone. When they discover Arthur's gone, they'll follow those tracks, and that'll buy us time. When you get far enough north, you find a way to break the trail off and cut back south. If you have those rawhide stockings on your horses they'll think he was taken by Indians—at least until it won't matter any more what they think."

Bellows was shaking his head. "That's crazy, going down that river in the dark. You taken a good look at it farther downstream? It's nothing but white water, tossing and twisting, like the snake it got its name from. Around here they call it 'the mad river.' You won't catch me trying that."

"It's been done," the colonel said. "Back in 'seventy-six an army exploring party went down it in boats, all the way down through Jackson Hole and through the Snake River Canyon. What was that lieutenant's name, Captain?"

"Doane, sir," Williams said. "Lieutenant Doane."

"That's right," the colonel said. "Lieutenant Doane. He took a party of six men down the river in boats, and they did it in winter. Doane was planning to explore the Snake from its source all the way to its mouth, but they had to give up just south of the Snake River Canyon."

"I don't wonder," Bellows said. "Sounds like this Lieutenant Doane was mad."

The colonel smiled. "He had more ambition than good sense, I'll grant you that. But the point is, they did it, and they survived. And they did it in winter. I think it was December by the time they finally gave it up. You'll be doing it in August, and for a distance of maybe twenty miles. At the rate of flow in most rivers, that should take you only about two hours."

"Don't make any difference," Bellows said, "two hours or two minutes. I've seen them rapids, and I don't want any part of going through 'em on a raft. You'd have Arthur to worry about, you'd be in the dark of night—you'd be looking to kill yourself."

"I don't know," Slocum said. "I think it's a good idea. It's the only way we can do it without leaving a trail for Arthur's people to follow."

"Exactly," the colonel said. "You think you can do it?"

"Sounds possible. If it gets us away clean, it's worth the risk."

"Good. When can you do it?"

"Tonight. The sooner the better."

"You're sure about that? You'll have to build the raft. I had Captain Williams bring enough rawhide

rope in his saddlebags to lash a thing like that together with, but it'll still take time. You'll have to
cut logs to the right length, drag them to a spot on
the river where you can work without being seen,
and get all your gear together. Can you do all that
before the lieutenant comes for Arthur's woman?''

"It's possible," Slocum said.

"We can do it," Bellows said. "I can build a
raft, but I'll be damned if I'll ride on it."

"I'll take the raft," Slocum said. "Bellows'll be
better at laying down trail, anyway. But we'll have
to know when and where to meet up with you."

The colonel glanced up at the sky. "It should be a
clear night. You'll be able to see the terrain you're
passing through. You got a watch?''

Slocum patted a vest pocket. "Won't do me any
good if it gets wet, but I can figure time without a
watch. You just give me a landmark to watch for,
and I'll know when I get there."

"I picked one out," the colonel said. "The river
runs pretty flat till it gets out of the Hole. Below
that it cuts down through some pretty steep bluffs.
When you get about twenty miles down, the bluff on
your right will break off sharply. There's a rocky
ledge that juts out from the end of it there. That's
where we plan to meet. You should be able to see it
from the river."

"What do I do when I get there?"

"I can't promise we'll be there when you do, but
there's a flat stretch of ground in a little pocket on
the east bank, just across from that ledge. You can
camp up there and wait for us. The river widens into
a pool there, and there's a ford just south of the
pool. We should meet up with you by dawn."

Slocum figured if things went right he ought to be there himself by two in the morning at the latest. And if the colonel's bunch had already picked the spot out, it shouldn't take them any four or five hours longer to show up. He was beginning to suspect the colonel was being cagey. Likely they wanted to see how things developed, make sure he'd gotten away clean, before they dealt themselves in. If it turned out Arthur's people got on his trail before then, the colonel would probably pull out and leave him and Bellows to face a rope all by themselves.

He was about to mention that little fact when a sudden thrashing came from behind him, and he turned to see the lieutenant clawing his way up through the brush.

"Patrol coming," the lieutenant said. "Up the ridge."

The colonel was on his feet. "How far?"

"Maybe two hundred yards." The lieutenant looked to have spent too much time behind a desk; he was having trouble getting his breath. "Should be here any minute."

The colonel seized the muzzle of his horse, laying a hand across its nostrils to keep it quiet. Slocum and the others leaped to their horses to do the same. Slocum watched the trees out the mouth of the ravine, but the brush was too thick to see ground, and he couldn't hear anything yet. He caught the lieutenant's eyes on him, but the lieutenant wasn't really seeing him. He was scared and listening, holding the bridle chains of his mount to keep them from jingling. Soon Slocum heard horses coming up the spine of the ridge, moving slowly, and then the barely audible murmur of men trading talk. He held to the bay's muzzle with one hand and slipped the Colt out of the holster with the other. There was enough brush on that ridge to make hoof tracks hard to see, but if those sentries were alert and looking they might pick them up, despite the rawhide stockings these horses were wearing. The voices grew a little louder, passed on by the mouth of the ravine, and then faded on up the ridge. He waited a long minute after they passed out of hearing, then reholstered the Colt.

They held the horses quiet for another five minutes, waiting to be sure the sentries were gone. Then the colonel untied his horse from its tree. "All right. The ridge should be clear for another hour or two, anyway. Captain, transfer that rawhide to Slocum's saddlebags, and let's get out of here before the next pair comes around."

When the rope was stowed in the bay's saddlebags, they led the horses down out of the ravine and mounted up. Slocum was surprised when the colonel leaned over to offer him his hand.

"Good luck," he said. "Keep your heads about you, and everything will go fine. We'll see you at the rendezvous site."

Slocum watched them go, three men in the uniforms of their country, riding out to meet other men bent on toppling their President. But he was feeling better. It was the waiting that got a man sweating. Once a job was really started, things settled into place and he could breathe again.

"We better split up soon as we get back," Bellows said. "Wouldn't do to have Troy come around wondering where both of us have gone off to. I'll scout out a place to build that raft and cut the logs so we'll have 'em ready to drag down there soon as night falls.''

"Let's get moving, then," Slocum said. "We're going to have a busy night, and we may be a little pressed for time.''

12

An hour after nightfall, Slocum and Bellows were down along the Snake at a little inlet about two miles below camp, the closest they could get and still feel safe from pickets. The inlet was shallow and surrounded on two sides by willows, leaving access to the water from a flat stretch of ground on the downriver side. They had dragged the logs by rope behind the horses down through the dark—thick lengths of lodgepole pine Bellows had cut that afternoon—and were working now to fashion them into the raft. It wasn't quite a clear night—the moon was going in and out of the clouds—but there was still plenty of light to see by.

Bellows was laying the logs out side by side so that the limbs he'd left on three of them stuck up in the right places. "This one here in the middle's the one you'll tie Arthur to," he said. "I left about two feet of it and carved a groove around it near the top. That ought to hold the rope tight. These two in back are for the steering poles and to brace yourself against." Edging the logs tight together, he lashed a small branch across the two vertical limbs at the back, forming a kind of backrest. The vertical limbs were lopped off about waist-high, each of them end-

ing in a V like a boy's slingshot: the remains of
forking branches Bellows had cut short. "You can
lay that long pole in this one here. I'll lash this other
one in place with the rawhide. I trimmed that wide
part flat at the base so you can use it as an oar."

Slocum was unraveling a thick coil of braided
rawhide rope, cutting it into long lengths and laying
them out on the ground. "Sounds all right. Let's
hope it works."

"I'm just glad it's you going to be doing this,
and not me," Bellows said.

"If I thought there was a better way of getting
him away from here, I wouldn't be doing it, either."

Bellows finished lashing the crude oar in its makeshift oarlock and came to help Slocum with the rope.
They cinched a noose tight around the end of an
outside log, wrapped the rope around the next in-
board log, pulled it up tight, and wrapped it around
the next, working from log to log, snugging them up
tight together.

"Well, you can't sink, anyway," Bellows said.
"Any water coming aboard will just run right back
through these cracks between the logs. It ain't like a
boat."

"Sinking's not what I'm worried about," Slocum
said. "It won't do me any good if the raft stays
afloat and I don't. If that river's as rough as you say
it is, it'll be all I can do to stay aboard. That's if the
raft don't hit a rock and break up under me."

"Colonel says that pissant lieutenant did it. If he
could do it, you can do it."

Slocum finished tying off the first length of rawhide, picked up another, and started winding it around

the outside log about six inches back from the first. "What's the odds on Arthur drowning? Going to be a lot of water coming back over here."

"Them rapids ain't constant. There's stretches of calm water between them. Raft'll go up and down when it hits them, anyway. He'll be able to catch enough breath if he keeps his head up."

"If he doesn't, I guess it won't matter if we hit a rock or not."

When they had the last length of rawhide wound through the logs and cinched up tight, Slocum stood back to look at the result. It didn't look like much in the moonlight: a makeshift raft about six feet by ten, with the two-foot limb sticking up in the middle and the crude backrest at the rear, the long oar lashed in the V of one of the uprights. It was solid enough—laced together at six-inch intervals from front to stern—but he had never done a thing like this, and he wasn't feeling too confident about it.

"Let's see if it works," he said. "Let's put it in the water."

Hoisting it at each end, they carried it down the bank and eased it into the water. Slocum tied a rope to one of the uprights at the rear and shoved the raft out into the inlet, the long oar trailing from its oarlock.

"Well, she floats," Bellows said.

Slocum reeled the raft in and handed the rope to Bellows. "Hang on to that. Let's see how she floats with me on her."

Holding to a willow branch, he stepped gingerly out on the raft. It sank a little under his weight, but it seemed steady enough.

"Give me that other pole."

Bellows handed him the long pole he planned to use to fend off rocks once he reached the rapids. He dug one end of it into the bank and pushed out into deeper water. The raft felt a little springy, the laced-together logs giving under his feet and flexing back up again as he moved. He figured that was all right; that would lend it some give when he hit that white water, and it ought to ride the waves better than a more solid raft would.

"It'll do," he said. "Pull me back in."

They tied the raft up close to the bank and cut enough willow branches to lay over it in case anybody happened this way. Slocum didn't think there was much danger of that, but he didn't want anything to go wrong this late in the game. When they were done, he pulled his watch from his vest pocket and angled it up to where he could see the face in the moonlight.

"We got time," he said. "Let's go check on those drunks in the bar tent."

They removed the rawhide stockings from the horses, stowed them in the saddlebags, and headed up the riverbank to the mouth of the Gros Ventre, where the pack animals were herded together in a rope corral. Right in camp the way it was, with water on two sides of it, the corral had so far gone unguarded; after checking to see that there were still no sentries posted, they crossed the Gros Ventre and cut back along the north bank till they were past the off-limits line. Then they forded the river again and rode back up into camp.

Campfires dotted the riverbank for a hundred yards

or more, illuminating the tents scattered through the trees. The smell of wood smoke was strong on the air, and a lazy buzz of talk rose from small knots of men gathered around the fires. The bar tent was in the middle of camp, large and noisy and lit with lanterns from within. A wide section of canvas was raised to form the entrance and let in air, but half the crowd had spilled out to do their drinking on the ground in front. Slocum and Bellows tied their horses to a picket stake and went inside.

The place was crowded and loud with talk, the smoke so thick it hurt the eyes. Several makeshift tables had been set up to accommodate card players, but there wasn't much sitting room; most of the men were bunched up around the tables or squatting on the ground along the canvas walls. Slocum and Bellows worked their way through the crowd to the bar, which was fashioned of canvas stretched taut over a skeleton of pine poles at the back, and ordered whiskey.

The drinks came in tin cups, but no one was likely to complain, since they were free. Slocum found an open space near one end of the bar and they hunkered down against a tent pole.

"Quite a crowd," Bellows said. "Things go right, there's enough to create a real commotion when the fun starts. A few Indian whoops around that corral and I figure all hell'll break loose."

"From the look of them, they'll be drunk enough by then," Slocum said.

The crowd was about half mule skinners and half cavalrymen, and the skinners looked to have got a head start on the troopers; a couple of them were already passed out in a corner. With the liquor free, most of the rest had taken a bottle apiece, so they wouldn't have to keep on making return trips to the bar. There were no officers in sight. The officers stuck to their own tents, where the drinking would be a little more refined.

"You sure you can stir this crowd up without getting yourself shot?" Slocum said. "You got to worry about the men around those tents too. It has to be done so nobody'll set out after you."

"You forget how long I worked with Indian scouts? I'm practically an Indian myself. I'll do it so they won't even know what started the commotion. By the time they figure out there ain't none of them mules missing, they'll think they was just hearing things."

"I'll take your word for it," Slocum said, "but I don't want you leading anybody to that raft."

"They won't even know I was there," Bellows said. "Don't worry about it. Where do you think we ought to go when this is all over?"

"Mexico. Head straight for Mexico and stay there. At least till we hear how things are working out back in this country."

Bellows was sloshing the whiskey around in his cup, gazing pensively off through the smoke. "I sure am going to miss that little Gloria. I ain't had me such a pretty little thing in many a year."

"Wait till you get to Mexico. With the money we'll be carrying, you'll have all the pretty señoritas you want."

Slocum was watching the crowd. All of them carried sidearms, but he couldn't see a rifle anywhere. That was a good sign, anyway; the corral was a good ways out of pistol range, and by the time these drunks got their feet going, Bellows ought to have done what he was there for and got away. But there were still those other men to worry about, the ones in the tents close to the corral. But if Bellows said he could do it so it wouldn't look suspicious, do it and get away clean, Slocum would just have to take him at his word. And it was time to get started; he'd seen all he'd come here to see.

He finished his whiskey and was starting to get to his feet when he became aware of a man looming over him, half drunk and swaying a little.

"Well, look who's here," the man said.

It was Ehrler, Bellow's former partner, the man Bellows had braced for his missing money in the army's mule corrals back in Green River. He had a bottle in one hand and a tin cup in the other, and the silly grin on his face showed he was well on his way toward joining those skinners passed out in the corners.

"I seen you two around camp," Ehrler said. "How come you never come over to visit? You got too fancy to associate with mule skinners?" He shouted over his shoulder. "Hey, Jones, here's the petticoat brigade! Come on over and get a whiff of the perfume."

"Shove off," Bellows said. "I told you I didn't want to see your ugly face again."

"Now is that friendly?" Ehrler said.

He swayed on his feet, that silly grin plastered to his face, a little whiskey spilling out of the cup hanging from his hand. Jones had turned from a crowd around one of the card tables, and the noise level in the tent had dropped off sharp. These men knew an insult when they heard one, and they were looking for a fight. Slocum got slowly to his feet, sensing Bellows doing the same beside him. He didn't want to fight in here; the whole crowd would pitch in, and that would foul things up for fair. Even if they didn't get themselves stomped, officers would come running, and they'd be half the night just sorting things out.

Ehrler swung half around to address the crowd, whiskey sloshing out of his cup. "You all know who this is. We're all working mules. These two is working mares. The two-legged kind. A couple of fancy-pants gents peddling women to the bigwigs."

Bellows was already going for his knife when Slocum hit Ehrler in the belly as hard as he could. Ehrler gagged and doubled over, and Slocum brought his knee up in the man's face, kicking him aside even as he started to go down. Jones had started to reach for his gun, but Slocum's upraised hand stopped him. It was half warning, half a move toward his own gun.

"I wouldn't do that," Slocum said. He scanned the crowd. Most of them had halted halfway up from their seats, stopped by the sight of Slocum's hand poised over his Colt. "Just a little private argument," he said. "Nothing to do with you. And now, if you'll just go back to your drinking, we'll be taking our leave. But don't move any too fast, or I might just shoot somebody by mistake."

Slowly, his hand hovering over his gun, he started working his way through the crowd. Jones backed out of his way, but the others stayed where they were, still in a half-crouch, watching him. He sensed Bellows close behind him, easing along backward to cover the rear. Nobody said anything, and by the time they reached the tent opening, the silence seemed louder than the noise had before. Slocum felt a hand touch his arm when he stepped outside, but he shook off the hand and the question the man was about to put to him. Then he was out in the open air, and the noise started up again inside the tent.

"What was that all about?" somebody said from the dark along the front of the tent.

"Nothing much," Slocum replied. "You want to find out, go in and ask somebody." By the time he got to his horse, the men outside were already jamming into the tent to get the news.

He untied the bay, watching the tent opening to make sure the traffic was all going in and none was coming out. "You think those two'll follow us?"

"Not likely," Bellows said. "You hit Ehrler a good one. Good thing, too—I was about to put my knife into him. But I know Ehrler. When he's pulled himself together, he'll do some big talking. And by the time he's done with talking he'll be too drunk to do anything else. He'd much rather fight a bottle than a man."

"Let's get away from here, just the same," Slocum said.

They rode back through camp at a trot, the noise from the bar tent gradually fading away behind. Little knots of men were still clustered around the campfires, and from somewhere back in the trees he heard a man squeezing out a tune on an accordion. He figured if they were lucky that little set-to with Ehrler might turn out in their favor. With those drunks already stirred up, it wouldn't take much more to set off a real disturbance.

Back at the tent area, he swung down off the bay and tied it to a wagon tongue. "I'm going to need a mount to carry Arthur on," he said. "Bring up one of them mules from the wagon teams. I borrowed a packsaddle and panniers from a skinner today. Told him I needed it to haul wood in. You'll find it in that wagon there. Get all the gear in there and I'll meet you out here in a few minutes."

He ducked into the tent he had been sharing with Laura Ryan. She was crouched by the Sibley stove, stoking the fire with a stick, wearing a shawl over her dress against the night's chill. When she saw him start to gather up his things, she pushed the stick into the stove and closed the hatch.

"It's tonight, then, is it?"

"Let's just say I won't be coming back." He lit a candle from a bunch she had brought along and started dripping wax onto the heads of a small fistful of matches, sealing them together until he figured they'd withstand water. "What time'd you say Arthur wanted his woman?"

"Lieutenant Troy said he would come for her at ten." She was watching his face, sober and quiet. "The other girls were already sent for. All but Judy. She's the one Arthur wants."

Finished with the matches, he stuck them down into a small leather pouch he'd made and closed it with a drawstring. Then he gathered up the buffalo robes from the willow branches they'd been using as a pallet and wrapped up everything inside the robes. "You'll have to sleep on that cot from here on."

"Alone too," she said.

"Afraid so. That won't make me happy, either.

But there's nothing for it." He tucked the bundle of robes under his arm and checked the tent to see if he'd forgotten anything. "Once they find Arthur's gone, and us with him, there'll be some pretty important people here asking questions about us. Don't let them scare you. As far as you know, we're just two men you hired on when we heard you were looking for guides back in Green River. As long as you stick to that story, they can't prove otherwise."

"I'll be all right," she said, still watching his face. "I don't scare easily."

"I didn't figure you would. You're an impressive woman. It's been a good trip."

"Good for me too."

She followed him out of the tent, the canvas flap closing off the light from inside. The moon was still going in and out of the clouds, but there were patches clear enough to see stars. He was beginning to feel keyed up, almost elated—the thing had started, and soon would be over with. Laura Ryan came to stand close to him and slipped something into his pocket.

"What's that?" he said.

"My card. It has my address on it. In case you ever come to Chicago."

"I doubt I'll ever get to Chicago, but you never can tell. Thanks. If I knew where I was going to be, I'd return the favor. Now, you better get back in the tent. Anybody sees you with us while we're leaving, it won't be easy explaining what you thought we were up to."

"Good luck—and be careful." She rose on tiptoe to give him a kiss. "Thanks for the adventure. I'll miss you on the rest of the trip." She ducked back into the tent.

Bellows was around the side of the tent, rigging up a mule with the packsaddle. He had already put rawhide stockings on all three animals. Slocum got a couple of army ration kits and a can of axle grease from the freight wagon, put them into the buffalo robe bundle with the matches and a change of clothes, and stashed the bundle in a pannier on the packsaddle. His war bag was already packed. He lashed it on behind the bay's saddle and tied the mule's halter rope to his saddle string.

"How much time we got?" Bellows said.

"About fifteen minutes till Troy gets here for the girl. Mrs. Ryan says he's taking Judy. The other girls are already gone."

"I know. I checked the tent. I didn't even get a chance to say goodbye to Gloria."

"Think about Mexico. Saying hello to all them pretty señoritas." He stuck his boot in the stirrup and swung up onto the bay. "Here, you better take my watch. From what I've seen, our Mr. Arthur is a very punctual man. Always keeps the girl with him for an hour. That means she'll be leaving the tent at about eleven-thirty. You give me about ten minutes—say, eleven-forty—and then set things going."

"What if he don't keep her an hour? Or keeps her longer?"

"Then I'll just have to play it as it goes and take my chances. You start things at eleven-forty. I'll worry about the rest of it."

"All right," Bellows said. "I'll meet you at the raft."

"If I ain't there on time, or if something goes

wrong and you get people after you, don't wait for me. I'll figure something out. Anyway, good luck, and I'll see you later.''

He touched spurs to the bay and headed for the ridge, starting up into the timber, the pack mule following along behind.

13

He climbed steadily up through the pines, past the place where they'd been cutting firewood when Williams had showed up that afternoon, and turned west along the spine of the ridge. The moon was burning a hole through a thin layer of clouds, lighting things up more than was comfortable. If Troop G's outriders sighted him here he could possibly talk his way clear, but likely they would take him down into camp to confirm who he was, and he couldn't afford the time that would take. He figured the risk was slight; that pair earlier in the day had been two ridges farther south, and he had no reason to believe they would change their circle for night patrol.

Soon the ridge began to slope downward and the fires of the main camp came in sight, scattered along the riverbank like so many ground-struck stars. He still had that keyed-up feeling, glad the waiting was over, glad to be moving. The night seemed to ring with silence, with only the steady plod of hooves on pine needles and the occasional raking of a branch along the mule's packsaddle to break the quiet. He was too far above camp to hear anything from there, but he figured those troopers and skinners should be working up a good drunk by this time. Now he could only hope they would react as he and Bellows expected.

He reined up where the ground began to drop away steeply in front of him and sat his horse for a moment, scanning the dark. The ridge bottomed out about thirty yards down, bending back south along the near edge of Arthur's private campsite. Through a patch of trees halfway between him and where the mule corral would be, he could see the lights of the bar tent, still too far away to hear much. When he was sure the area was clear, he dismounted and led the bay down through the pines to the vantage point he had picked out the night before.

From here he could see the sentry along the northern edge of the rope perimeter around Arthur's tent site. He was about forty yards to the right of the man, which would keep him clear of the sentry on the east side. It was the man on the north he was interested in; that was the stretch Troy would take the girl through.

Either he was early, or Troy was late; the regular sentry was still there, leaning up against a tree the rope was tied to. Slocum tethered the bay to a pine and crouched down to wait.

He could see the glow of campfires off through the trees to his right and the occasional vague shape of a man passing in front of a fire. Somebody was splitting up some firewood over there, but the distance was too great to hear anything else. He saw the flare of a match as the sentry lit a smoke, and then the tiny glow of the cigarette after the match went out. That was unusual; usually the man started diligently pacing off his beat when Troy was due to arrive.

By the time the sentry had smoked the cigarette down and ground it out under his boot, Slocum was beginning to think something must have gone wrong. Unless his sense of time was failing him, Troy should have been here by now. Maybe Arthur had changed his mind. If this day was like the rest, he had spent it fishing, and maybe he'd decided he was too tired for frolic. Maybe the novelty of a different woman every night had grown thin. The man wasn't young, and likely the body wasn't as willing as the mind wanted to think. If that was the case, the whole thing had gone sour. They would have to call it off, meet up with the colonel at the rendezvous point in the morning without the prize they were supposed to bring along, and make new arrangements. The colonel wouldn't be happy about that, and neither would Slocum. He wanted this thing over and done with. And unless he got to Bellows in time to stop him, Bellows would create that diversion for nothing, and they wouldn't be able to use the trick a second time.

He was still debating what to do when he saw somebody coming through the trees from the direction of camp and recognized the stolid form of Lieutenant Troy.

The sentry came to attention and saluted when Troy approached him. Troy conferred with him briefly, and then the sentry saluted again and started off toward the bar tent. Slocum wondered what had been said, how Troy had explained the man's being relieved every night at the same time. From what Ehrler had said in the bar tent, it was clear that everybody knew about the women, but likely the army would have some cover story to keep up pretenses. Troy went along the rope perimeter, checking the rope line and the cowbells, scanning the surrounding area. Satisfied that everything was in order, he set off through the dark in the direction of the woman's camp. Slocum waited until he was out of sight, then crept down the last little slope of the ridge, pausing behind every other tree to watch and listen.

He reached the perimeter without mishap and sheltered behind another tree, his eyes searching the dark. Still no sign of trouble. The rope stretched about knee-high from tree to tree. Careful not to set the cowbells to jingling, he stepped over it and ducked into some bushes on the other side.

He should be safe from sight here. The rope enclosure had been made especially large to protect Arthur's privacy, and those sentries were supposed to guard the perimeter, not keep an eye on things inside it. Still, he didn't like to take chances. Moving low and quiet, he slipped from bush to bush, from tree to tree, till Arthur's tent came in sight— dark, sheltered in a little semicircle of brush, the opening facing east toward the ridge.

He watched it for a minute or two. Arthur would be lying awake in there. Carefully, he skirted the tent and crouched down in the brush where he could see the opening.

The tent flap was closed. There was no sign of life, and no lantern was lit inside. Either Arthur was worried about privacy or he liked his women in the dark, but whichever was the case, it made this job easier. A lantern inside would have lit him up when that tent flap was opened.

Twenty minutes later, he heard the tinkle of a cowbell back where he had crossed the perimeter. From previous nights' watching, he knew what that was: Troy untying the rope so Judy wouldn't have to step over it in her robe; every night that he had stood watch, Troy had brought the girl already in a robe. Maybe Arthur didn't like to work his way through all those clothes. Or maybe the girls found dressing after things were over too difficult in the dark confines of a tent. He worked his way farther back into the brush and waited.

Soon he saw them coming out of the dark. Judy's pale blonde hair hung down to her shoulders and an even paler robe was belted around her waist. The darker form of the lieutenant was beside her. Judy was clutching the robe tight to her throat, stepping delicately along in little flat-heeled slippers, the lieutenant holding her arm with the uncomfortable look of a man in an awkward situation he didn't really know how to handle. They halted about ten yards from the tent; Troy said something too low to make out, patted Judy reassuringly on the arm, and turned back the way he had come. Judy paused for a moment, as if working up her nerve, then came on toward the tent.

She stopped at the tent opening and fluffed out her hair—that woman's instinct to pretty herself up, even though it would be too dark in there for Arthur to see. She glanced quickly around as if to make sure no one was watching, then started undoing her belt. Slocum's breath caught in his throat when he saw what she was doing: the robe fell to her waist, revealing her slim back pale in what little moonlight there was. Then she shucked out of the sleeves and stood there totally naked, long legs spread slightly apart, folding the robe up in her hands. She parted the tent flap with one hand, her large breasts jiggling as she bent to toss the robe into the tent. A mur-

mured voice came from within, and she laughed and ducked inside.

Slocum found he'd been holding his breath. Through the tent wall he heard Arthur murmur something else, and Judy's giggled reply. He was suddenly embarrassed to be where he was, privy to the fumbling fondlings of a man with a whore in his tent, a personage few people thought of as a man with needs like any other. There was something about lurking out here in the dark, with Arthur not knowing he was being spied on, that left a bad taste in his mouth. He tried to concentrate on something else.

The moon was still burning a small hole through the clouds. The distant sounds of someone splitting firewood had ceased. The rope perimeter was too far away to see, but Troy should be pacing back and forth over there, serving as sentry until it was time for him to escort Judy back to her tent. He wondered if Troy was bothered, the way he was, by the thoughts of what was going on in there. But Troy wasn't close enough to hear any sounds. He set his mind on what he would do with his twenty-five thousand dollars when he and Bellows got paid off, and shut his ears to the sounds. It was going to be a long wait.

He had most of the money spent by the time he heard the rustle of the tent flap and saw Judy emerge into the moonlight, the robe already belted around her. He hadn't been too successful at blocking out sounds from within the tent, but most of it had been talk after the first few minutes, not loud enough to make out. Judy paused to fix herself up, running her hands through her hair, cinching the belt up tighter.

Then she set off toward where Troy would be wait-ing, gradually fading into the dark.

Slocum figured she'd been in there about the usual hour, but unless he was wrong, Troy had been late in bringing her. Bellows might be starting his diver-sion any minute. The best way would have been to wait until Arthur was asleep, but that was impossi-ble; he would have to go in after him, and that would mean moving fast enough to find the man in the dark of the tent and knock him out before he had time to call for help. And that was not going to be easy.

He was drawing his Colt when the tent flap rustled again and Arthur stepped outside.

He looked tousle-haired and sleepy, his pale legs barely showing under a dark robe he had belted around his middle. Slocum froze where he was, scarcely even breathing, but Arthur was too preoc-cupied to notice anything amiss. He rounded the near corner of the tent and stood facing away, spraddle-legged. Soon Slocum heard the faint sounds that told him Arthur was urinating.

Arthur finished and belted up his robe. Slocum watched, his Colt out, waiting. When Arthur bent to duck back into the tent, Slocum slipped quickly up behind him and clipped him hard just above the ear.

Arthur grunted and started to go down, already out. Slocum caught him and eased him to the ground, scanning the dark, listening. There was no sign that anybody had heard. He searched for Arthur's pulse. The man was out cold, but he was all right. Slocum holstered the Colt and crept into the tent, feeling around in the dark for what clothes he could find. Likely Arthur was going to get drenched on that raft, and unless he had some dry clothes after they'd got ashore, he might not survive the night. Working quickly, he gathered up what little he could find, wrapping it all up in one of Arthur's blankets and tying it together with a length of rawhide rope from his own pocket. He lashed the little bundle to his belt and ducked back outside.

Arthur was still lying on his side, one arm flung out. There was still no sign of any reaction from the perimeter or of Bellows's diversion. Slocum figured he had maybe ten minutes left before Troy returned. What with Troy being late, they were cutting it very fine. Bellows might start things going any moment. He bent to sling Arthur up over his back. He was a heavy man; too much rich eating back there in the East. Slocum began moving awkwardly back toward the northern edge of the enclosure.

Troy hadn't got back yet. The rope perimeter was still clear, but with Arthur on his back, he was too unsteady to risk stepping over it and setting those cowbells off. He eased Arthur to the ground, stepped across, and dragged the heavy man through under the rope. He had just got him hoisted onto his back again when he heard the first shot from the direction of the bar tent.

He froze for a moment, his head turned that way. The shot had quickly grown to a volley, rapid bursts of fire that had a sound of panic in it, like men firing at things they couldn't see. Now he heard shouts from the main camp, and through the trees he could see the thin shapes of men passing in front of camp-fires at a run. Hoping Bellows knew what he was doing, he started trotting heavily along the perimeter, aiming for the shelter of those trees up on the ridge.

He hadn't gone twenty yards when he heard somebody running through the brush along the bottom of the ridge. He hit the ground without thinking, Arthur's heavy weight landing crushingly on his back, and rolled to put himself on top. He hugged the ground, risking just enough of a look to see another sentry break out into the open ahead of him, running toward the commotion at the bar tent. The man was levering a round into his carbine as he ran, and Slocum had one quick thought about Troop G's poor leadership. Those sentries should have been told to stay at their posts no matter what. Then the man was gone, and Slocum dragged Arthur up across his shoulders again and struggled on up the slope.

He was fighting for his breath by the time he reached the bay. He shrugged Arthur off his shoulders, slinging him face down across the back of the pack mule, and went to lashing the man's hands and feet to a cord cinched up tight under the mule's belly. The mule shied and jerked at its lead rope, and he had to hit it on the nose to get it to stand still. Arthur was still out; a tap that hard should keep him out for quite a while. The firing from the bar tent had begun to taper off, and he could hear faint shouts as somebody—likely an officer—tried to bring things under control. He didn't take time to stow the bundle of Arthur's clothes, just untied the bay and swung up into the saddle with it still dangling from his belt. Curbing an urge to use the spurs, he started at a fast walk south along the butt of the ridge. Time enough for a faster pace when he was sure all those sentries were gone.

He cut wide around the southern edge of Arthur's enclosure, scanning the dark for any sign of another sentry. This post too had been deserted. He kept the horse at a walk until he was past the far corner of the perimeter. Then he spurred it into a trot, angling southwest toward that little inlet where the raft was.

He barely heard the riders coming in time to rein up. They were slashing through the brush on his left, and he swung quickly down out of the saddle to give a lower silhouette, holding to the bay's muzzle to keep it quiet. They passed him at a run, scarcely twenty yards ahead, two troopers with their carbines out, raking their mounts with the spurs. That was good; the commotion was drawing the outriders in as well. When he was sure they were out of hearing, he mounted up again and kicked the bay into a run.

He made it to the inlet without sighting any more troopers and vaulted from the saddle to tie the bay's reins to a willow alongside the raft. Quickly, he scooped off the willow branches they'd laid over the raft for cover. He was cutting the cords holding Arthur on the mule when he heard a splashing coming down along the near edge of the river and saw Bellows's paint approaching at a canter. Bellows jumped to the ground and helped him to lower Arthur carefully off the mule.

"Went like a stage play," he said. "Everybody knew his part. I hadn't hardly got things started when them drunks came busting out of that tent, shooting at anything that moved. Killed a good dozen mules that I could see, and I want you to know I was already hightailing it out of there."

There was no more firing coming from the camp. The officers must have got things under control. No telling what they were doing now. "Pull that raft up close to the bank," Slocum said. "We got to move fast. It'll take 'em a while trying to figure out what the hell happened, but we can't take a chance on them deciding to fan out and search the area."

While Bellows held the raft steady, Slocum lugged Arthur aboard and tied his hands to the upright in the middle, pulling the rope tight so it held the man's head up off the logs a little. He left the legs untied; he wanted Arthur free to manuever after he came to. Otherwise, he might drown. Then he went to the pack mule to retrieve the buffalo-robe bundle he'd put together in Laura Ryan's tent.

"Give me your knives," he said. "I keep mine in my boot, and I might lose them boots if we get dumped. And you can take this Colt. Things go right, I won't need it, and I don't want it getting soaked in the river."

He untied the buffalo-robe bundle and stashed Arthur's clothes inside. When he had the bundle lashed up tight again—fur side in, hide side out—he took the can of axle grease he'd brought from the wagon and started smearing the grease over the hide, caking it up thick. That would keep it as waterproof as possible. Then he fastened a long rawhide rope to the lashings of the bundle and tied the other end of it around his ankle.

"What's that for?" Bellows said.

"I don't want to try hanging on to more than one thing if we go in that river. I'll have my hands full with Arthur. This way, if we make it ashore, we might have some dry clothes and rations, anyway." He unbuckled his gunbelt, pulled off his boots, and handed them to Bellows. "Stow this stuff in one of those panniers on the mule. And you better make it to that rendezvous soon as you can, 'cause I don't want to go bare any longer than I have to.''

"I'll make it," Bellows said. "You just worry about that river."

Slocum strapped one of Bellows's knives to his belt and dropped the other one in its sheath and sling down the back of his neck. He tossed the grease-smeared bundle out onto the raft and stepped off the bank after it. Bellows handed him the long pole and pushed the raft out into deeper water, only the rope tied to a willow holding it close to the bank.

"I may not get there till morning," Bellows said. "I figure to lay tracks north about four hours. Then I'll have to cut back and work my way back down without leaving sign. That'll take a while."

"Just make it as fast as you can. I don't want to face the colonel's bunch by myself if I can help it. Especially without my boots and gun."

Bellows untied the rope from the willow and Slocum dug the pole into the bottom, pushing himself out into the Snake.

14

He felt the pull of the river as soon as he was out of the inlet.

The raft slowed for a moment as the current hit the upstream corner. Then the back end began to swing around in the calmer water at the rear, starting a circle that threatened to take him out of control. He braced his feet in the crevices between the logs and found bottom with the long pole, working against the current until he had the raft headed in the right direction, out in the river and being carried swiftly downstream. He looked back once, but Bellows was already out of sight.

The moon had broken through the clouds again, and in the sudden light he could see the sweep of water ahead of him, bright against the darker bulk of the trees along the banks. The river was fairly wide here, running fast, but with no rocks or boulders showing. Above him on the west, the Tetons loomed, jagged and black, blocking out the sky. He laid the pole in its rest atop the first of the two limbs Bellows had left jutting up at the rear and took hold of the oar lashed in place in the second.

The sounds of the encampment had dropped away behind him. All he could hear now was the quiet rush of the water and the splash of the long oar as he worked it like a rudder, trying to keep the raft headed straight. Those troopers back there should still be sorting things out. It ought to take them a while to make sure there wasn't anything for those drunks to be shooting at, but when they did he hoped they would all go back to bed.

With the rope perimeter still secure around Arthur's tent area, there would be no reason for them to suspect anything was amiss. And surely none of them would take it in his head to brief the President about a little thing like some drunks shooting at sounds in the night. One thing he had learned from listening around among the troopers was that nobody wanted to be the one to disturb the President unless it was absolutely necessary. If he was lucky, they wouldn't even know the man was gone till late in the morning, when somebody would begin to wonder why he hadn't showed up for breakfast. And Slocum hoped to turn him over to the colonel, get his pay, and be gone long before that happened.

Arthur looked to be still unconscious. He lay on his belly on the raft like a calf trussed for branding, legs sprawled wide, arms pulled up by the thongs binding his wrists to that limb jutting up from the center log. The water licking up through the cracks between the logs was already beginning to wet the edges of his dressing gown, but he was all right. The test would come when they hit rougher water; that would bring him to. At least Slocum hoped it would, because the man would have to fend for himself then, would have to be able to keep his head up for air. When that water started rushing back over the raft, Slocum would have his own hands full just trying to keep them headed straight, trying to stay on his feet and fend off any boulders which loomed up in their path.

The current here seemed pretty manageable, but Bellows had called the Snake "the mad river," and Bellows usually knew what he was talking about. Slocum didn't want to think of what that might mean. If the raft started breaking up beneath them he would have to cut Arthur loose, and he wasn't sure he could do that and save himself at the same time.

So far things were going all right. He kept the oar working, staying in the middle of the channel cut by the current. No rocks or rapids yet, but both Bellows and the colonel had said the river wouldn't narrow for several miles downstream. It was running fairly straight now, and he lifted the oar in its makeshift oarlock, letting the raft drift on the current, and looked up at the sky. He could see a few stars in the hole burned through the clouds by the moon. Except for the rush of the river, the night seemed very quiet. For a moment, the fact of what he was doing hit him very strangely: he was alone at night on a fast-running river under a spotty sky in the middle of nowhere, with the President of the United States tied in his nightshirt and dressing gown to a limb in the center of a makeshift raft, unconscious and headed for God knew what. But he blocked it all out of his mind and bent his weight to the oar again.

They drifted for what seemed at least an hour, the river winding in wide, sweeping turns down through the valley, Slocum occasionally working the oar to prevent the start of a sideways swing. Soon he sensed the bulk of a mountain looming up ahead to the east, and then the riverbed began to narrow and heavily timbered bluffs sloped up on either side. Now boulders began to appear out of the moonlight ahead and he took up the long pole, preparing to fend them off. The raft was still riding steadily on the current with just a little water washing over the prow.

Then, up ahead, Slocum began to hear the rising roar of white water.

He gripped the pole, straining to see where the sound was coming from. For a long minute he could see only the straight stretch of river. Then he saw where the channel began a sharp bend to the right, dropping abruptly down into a narrow boil of rapids between two large slabs of rock jutting out from the bank on either side, then swirling in a wild curve back to the left beyond the rocks. He lurched as the raft dipped beneath him, gaining speed now, being drawn rapidly toward that slab of rock coming at him on the right. He wedged his feet in the cracks between the logs, bracing himself against the limb lashed across the two upright branches at his back, the long pole raised chest-high, his arms tensed for the shock he knew was coming.

The raft plunged into a boiling trough, a wave of white water rushing back over it, almost sweeping him off his feet, but he rocked with it as it rose on the next swell, sliding sideways now, heading directly for that looming slab of rock. He barely got the pole on the rock before the raft hit it.

A wave of water struck him from the rear. The raft had rammed the rock sideways and stuck, held there by the force of the current. He felt the offshore side begin to go under, beaten down by the relentless weight of water pouring over it. Only the hold of his feet in the cracks kept him aboard as he fought furiously with the pole, trying to push away from the bank.

There was no give. It was like trying to hold a locomotive off by hand. He felt the raft lurch beneath him, slanting deeper, the rushing rapids sucking it down, and he plunged the pole underwater near the right rear corner, striking what he'd hoped to find: underwater rock. He leaned all his weight on the pole and felt the raft begin slowly to move, scraping inch by inch along the rocky bank, the river surging up to his knees, pulling at him, threatening to dislodge him. Then the current lifted the raft from the rear and swept them away, plunging and rising, the logs flexing under his feet. For a heartbeat or two he was too busy fending off the boulders to be sure they'd made it; then the raft rose over a final roiling swell and they were clear, around the bend and into another channel, still narrow and faster than before, but running straight again.

He was drenched to the thighs and splattered by the spray from there up. The bundle he'd lashed to his leg had been washed overboard; he could feel the rawhide rope tugging at his ankle, and he looked back to see the end of it submerged, plowing through white water. Then the bundle leaped into sight, skipping and splashing along on the surface, and he turned back to the front.

Arthur had been tossed onto his back, his robe splayed open and held only by the cord around his middle. The white nightshirt was bright in the moonlight. He was wet through, but conscious now, his wide eyes blinking back water and staring at Slocum as if in a nightmare. Those eyes flicked to the water splashing up around him, to the dark banks fleeing past on either side and the moon overhead. He tried to work his mouth, but nothing came out, and Slocum knew he was too shocked and stunned to take in what was happening. Then they were coming up on another stretch of white water, boiling around a section of bank reaching out into the river from the left, and he forgot about Arthur and hefted the pole again.

Again there was that sudden swift pull to the right, the raft skidding sideways and heading for the bank. The nose went under so far that the wave washing back over it put Arthur completely out of sight, but this time there was no rock on the right bank, and Slocum found bottom with his pole, working it rapidly and rhythmically like a man rowing a canoe, bringing them around with the current, bracing himself as the raft leaped and plunged and water came rushing back over him. The nose went up like a bronc trying to unseat its rider, crested the swell, and dived again. When it came back up, he saw Arthur being twisted about by the waves like a streamer in the wind, clutching to the limb he was tied to, scrambling to keep from being dragged over the side. Then they were out of these rapids too, rocking and buffeting along on the current, the white water behind them.

Arthur had ended up on his side. He twisted himself over onto his back, trying to kick himself up on his hams. He got a knee under him, flung a glance at the river up ahead, and turned to shout at Slocum.

"What . . ." was all he could get out; he seemed too stunned to put a sentence together, and he gave it up, clinging to his limb, white-faced, as he watched the water rush past.

Slocum tried to ignore him, concentrating on the next stretch of rough water approaching, trying to judge how far ahead it was and which way the river would turn, and whether it would be rougher than the rapids they'd already passed through. He didn't like the sound of it. The roar of white water was louder than any he'd heard so far, and the river was already beginning to narrow, sucking the raft along faster and faster. The bluffs had closed in on both sides, rising almost straight up from the banks, and the only stretch of sky was a narrow streak over-head, almost as narrow as the river.

Arthur was struggling now; he rolled over onto his belly and worked himself up onto his knees, facing forward, the drenched robe clinging to his rump. He seemed to be staring at that white water up ahead, and when he turned, Slocum could see by his eyes that he had finally come all the way to. For the first time it had sunk in that he was really out here and this was really happening. He started to shout some-thing, but the raft hit the first of the swells before he could get the words out, a big wave surging back over him, sweeping him from his knees, stringing him out at the end of his rope again.

The water hit Slocum like an avalanche. He felt his feet go out from under him and he dropped the pole, grabbing for the makeshift oarlock to keep himself aboard. The raft bucked and plunged, going so far under that for an instant the water was over his head. It surged back up with such force that he was driven to his knees, and he barely had his eyes clear when he saw a huge rock dead ahead, rushing to-ward them like the prow of a ship.

There was nothing he could do but hold on.

The raft smashed into the rock with a splintering and crunching of wood. The impact nearly jerked him loose. It was a second or two before he got his wits back, and when he did he could feel the raft beginning to break up under him. The nose had climbed halfway up the rock. The logs had split apart and were threatening to give way entirely. The current was forcing the back end under, and the water was already up to his knees. He had to act now or it would be too late. He drew his knife, let go of the oarlock, and leaped for Arthur.

He landed on the man's back, clinging to the dressing gown with one hand while he sought the rope with the knife. One fast slice and Arthur was free. Then the river rolled over them, sweeping them off what was left of the raft, around the rock, and into the roiling rapids.

Arthur's wrists were still bound together. Slocum let the knife go, holding to the collar of the robe as the undertow sucked them down. They were caught in some kind of whirlpool just beyond the rock, where the rapids spilling out of the narrow channel met the calmer water below. Every time they started to rise toward the surface, Slocum felt another churning swirl buffet them under again. For a moment he was afraid they were going to drown. Then he felt the pull of the undertow slacken, and suddenly his head was above water and he was gasping for air.

They were being swept rapidly downstream now. Arthur was still struggling in his grasp, but Slocum managed to hold the President's head above water. They were face to face, Arthur's terrified eyes only inches from his own, his teeth clenched, his skin white and icy. Slocum craned his neck to see where the river was taking them, but all he could see was water and the dark bluffs on either side. They were swept around another boulder in midstream. Then Slocum saw a wide bend to the right coming up ahead, and he began to kick with the current, trying to make it into the lee of the bank on the left.

Arthur seemed to come to his senses. Now he too began to kick feebly, clutching Slocum's collar. Slocum felt the drag of the current leave him, and he kicked on harder, swimming with one hand now, dragging Arthur with the other. He pushed off a rock and felt himself being carried into calmer water. The bundle at the end of its rope still tugged at his ankle. Finally he felt rocky bottom underfoot, and struggled a ways farther until his hand hit bottom too. He splashed on until he could get to his feet, dragged Arthur up, and together they staggered out of the river and collapsed on a rocky little strip of bank.

He lay there for what seemed a long time, coughing and gasping for air. He could hear Arthur coughing too, but he sounded no worse off. He had a hard time getting his mind to work, and it was finally the cold that forced him up off his back.

Arthur saw him move; those frightened eyes flicked toward him, but he only rose to a sitting position, still struggling to get his wind back, trying to figure out where they were.

Steep, timbered bluffs still lined both sides of the river. There was no sign of that rocky ridge the colonel had told him about, with its distinctive outstretched escarpment. The bluffs had been with them for all the last stretch of the river, and he figured the colonel's rendezvous point was still farther south, downriver. That meant a long walk in the cold night, and if they didn't get into warmer clothes they would die of the chill. He felt around for the rawhide rope lashed to his ankle, pulled the hide-wrapped bundle up out of the shallows, and was relieved to find it was still intact.

He retrieved the second knife from the sheath on its string down the back of his neck and cut the rope from his ankle. Then he cut the lashings of the bundle and laid the buffalo robes open and felt around the stuff he'd stashed inside. A little water had leaked in in a place or two, but the clothes were dry enough. He dragged himself to his feet and went over to where Arthur lay.

"Get up," he said. "We got traveling to do."

Arthur looked up at him. "Where? Why?"

"'Cause you're going to die of the cold if you don't move. Other than that, it's not my business to tell you." He cut the robe binding Arthur's wrists together and sheathed the knife. "Get out of that robe. I got some dry clothes for you. And there's no sense trying to get away. I'm the only chance you got to stay alive. So just stick where you are."

Back at the bundle, he sorted through what he had till he found the clothes he'd taken out of Arthur's tent: pants, shirt, some kind of vest, and jacket. The man would have to do without underclothes or shoes, and they could use those buffalo robes to keep warmer. He turned back to see that Arthur had stripped and was standing there white and naked and shivering, covering himself with the saturated robe.

He carried the dry clothing over to Arthur and took the wet robe and nightshirt from him. "Here. Get into these. When you're dressed, we're going to move."

Slocum got out of his own wet clothes and into the ones he'd stashed in the bundle. He'd lost his socks in the river—the current had stripped them right off him—but Arthur was going to have to manage barefoot too. The matches were all right, still encased in the wax in the little leather sack he'd made. He stuck the sack in the pocket of his dry pants, then tied the wet things up with the rations in another little bundle and took one of the buffalo robes back to Arthur.

Arthur was dressed, but he was still shivering. He still looked scared and subdued, as if realizing the helpless position he was in, and he made no protest when his wrists were bound together again. Slocum draped the buffalo robe over him—greasy hide out, fur side in—and tied it across his shoulders like a cape. Then he draped the other robe over his own shoulders and tugged at the rope attached to Arthur's wrists.

"Come on. We got some walking to do."

Arthur didn't look happy, but he moved and he didn't say anything. Slocum got up into the trees, where the soft ground would be easier on their feet, following the river, watching the line of the other bank. The colonel had said a raft should cover about ten miles in an hour, and he knew they'd been more than an hour in the river. Figure two hours altogether, with the time just spent on the bank, and that would put them something short of twenty miles downstream. The colonel's rendezvous point couldn't be too far ahead.

After half an hour they still hadn't reached it. His feet were cold and were beginning to hurt in a place or two where he'd struck a rock in the river, but the walking was keeping him warm enough. Arthur had said nothing in all that time, just followed along behind, occasionally slipping on the slope when the ground gave beneath him. Twice Slocum had had to go back and drag him to his feet, but there'd been no talk then, either. He had no idea what was going on in the man's mind—if he was still too stunned to think, or if he was brooding over his situation, trying to figure some way out of it—but it didn't matter. The colonel would take charge of him soon, and then this thing would be done, and Slocum would be out of it.

He figured it was another half hour before the bluffs began to peter out along the far bank and he saw the end of the ridge the colonel had told him about. It was a long, rocky ledge reaching out from the hillside, silhouetted against the moonlit sky. Towing the silent Arthur behind him, he angled down the slope until he found the grassy bank, where the colonel had said it would be: a little open area like a half-moon on the near side of the river. He came out of the tree line, dropped the little bundle of wet clothes, and scanned the terrain.

There was no sign of the colonel, but there was no telling when he would show. Before dawn, Slocum hoped. Arthur was standing like a dumb ox at the end of his rope, watching him. Slocum tied the rope to a small tree and set about finding enough dry wood along the bank to build a fire. This was pretty deserted country, and they were a long way downstream; if things had gone right, he could risk a fire. He wasn't about to spend the rest of the night cold and damp, with only a buffalo robe to keep him warm.

Arthur was sitting beside the tree he was tied to, clutching the buffalo robe over his shoulders, his head down on his knees. When Slocum had gathered enough wood, he laid it in a small circle close to the tree so he wouldn't have to move the man again. He dug a match out of the wax and struck it on a rock, blowing on the dried ferns and leaves he'd laid under the wood. When he was sure the fire had caught and was going to burn, he looked up to see Arthur watching him.

For a long moment Arthur didn't say anything. He studied Slocum's face with a vacant expression. Finally he opened his mouth, but all that came out was a croak. He got himself under control and tried again. "What's going to happen to me?"

"You ain't going to be hurt," Slocum said. "Least not by me. There's just some people who want a little parley with you. Now you better try to get some sleep."

Arthur still seemed a little vacant, as if he couldn't get his mind to take all this in. Likely he was exhausted; his face was pale and drawn, with heavy bags under the eyes, and he was shivering. He dragged himself over to lie down by the fire, wrapped in the buffalo robe. The strain seemed to catch up to him pretty fast; in only a minute or two, he was asleep.

Slocum unraveled the wet clothes, draped them on a bush to dry, and hung what was left of his bundle— mostly army rations now—from a tree limb to keep it out of reach of predators. Then, with the second buffalo robe, he laid himself a bedroll across the fire from Arthur. He wasn't worried that the man would get himself free: that was rawhide rope he was using and, wet as it had been, the knots would be unworkable now that they had dried. He was tired and drained himself, and he wanted a smoke, but tobacco was the one thing he'd forgotten to put in that bundle, and he'd lost his makings in the river.

He hoped the colonel got here before too long—and Bellows too—but he wasn't going to be able to keep awake waiting for them. He tugged the robe closer around him, edged up nearer to the fire and tried to go to sleep.

15

Slocum woke with the first faint light of dawn. He had slept fitfully, waking every hour or so to feed the fire. Several times during the night he had heard Arthur tossing and turning in his sleep, once muttering to himself, but never really coming awake. He was still asleep now, his bound hands bunched up under his chest, the buffalo robe worked down around his waist by all that restless turning. Slocum rose from his bedroll and crossed to pull the robe back up over the man's shoulders.

A sudden noise from across the river brought him around to see two elk, a bull and a cow, trotting up a grassy clearing from where they'd been drinking at the water's edge. They disappeared into the trees running north along that rocky ridge he'd used as a landmark the night before. The clearing on the opposite bank was about a hundred yards wide, reaching up over the crest of a small hill below the ledge thrusting out at the south end of the ridge. The river looked shallow here, with a thin wisp of fog lying along the surface of it. There was still no sign of Bellows or the colonel. He went to the river to get himself a drink, then rustled up some more wood for the fire.

When he had the fire going again, he saw that Arthur was awake. He cut down the little bundle he'd hung from the tree limb and brought an issue of rations over to where the man lay watching him.

"I'm going to cut your hands loose," he said, "but I don't advise trying anything. You couldn't overpower me, and likely you'd die out here by yourself even if you could. So I suggest you just sit up and eat this."

When his hands were free, Arthur sat up and began massaging his wrists. He was watching Slocum, as if to see what manner of man this was who had snatched him from his tent and nearly drowned him in the dead of night. "Why?" he said.

" 'Cause you'll starve if you don't," Slocum said. "It's been a cold, wet night for both of us. You need some food in your belly."

"Why am I here?"

"That's something I'd rather not talk about. It's not my affair. Right now, you better get over here by this fire and warm yourself up."

Arthur looked as if he wanted to pursue the question, but something in Slocum's face must have told him it wouldn't do him any good. He dragged himself over closer to the fire and pulled the robe around him, digging gingerly around in the ration kit Slocum had handed him.

"What is it?" he said.

"Hardtack," Slocum said. "A little salt pork, I expect."

Arthur tried a bite of the salt pork and made a face. "It's hardly what I would call edible."

"It's what you feed your soldiers when they're in the field. That's regular army issue."

"I don't suppose you would have some coffee?"

"Should be an ounce of army-issue Santos coffee in that ration kit, but we got nothing to brew it in. I didn't bring any coffee pot with me. You'll just have to make do with what we have."

Slocum hunkered down beside the fire and tried some of the hardtack. As Arthur had said, it was hardly what a man would call edible, and he too was sorry they had no coffee. The only way to eat hardtack—the way most of the troopers ate it—was to bust it up on a rock with a gun butt and soften it in a pot of coffee. Otherwise it could break a man's teeth just trying to get a bite.

Arthur was trying to get some of the pork down, nibbling at it as if he could barely stand the taste. He looked a sight. His hair was twisted into a fright wig by the way it had dried while he slept, and his burnsides and moustache looked stiff and straggly. The fact that he'd slept in his clothes didn't help, and Slocum saw now that the vest he'd dragged out of the tent was the one Arthur wore when he was fishing; he could see fishhooks and leaders and line peeking out of the little pockets across the front of it. The man didn't look like much now; certainly he didn't look like the leader of a country. He was just a fat, tired man well past his prime, still recovering from an experience which must have taken at least a year off his life.

He was studying Slocum's face as he ate. After a while he gave up on the pork and tossed what remained of it into the fire. "You're the man I met the other day," he said. "The one who stopped that drunken Indian. You saved my life. Why did you do this—bring me out here like this?"

"I took care of that Indian because he was about to kill you. I'd do the same for any man. This other thing is something different. And, like I said, it's not really my affair."

"I take it that means you were hired to do this."

"I told you I'd rather not talk about it."

"And since you haven't killed me—since you went to some length to get me out of that river, when it would have been easier to let me drown and save yourself—I assume you're supposed to deliver me to whoever hired you."

"That's about it."

Arthur tried some of the hardtack, but one bite put another sour look on his face. He tossed it into the fire after the pork. "You couldn't perhaps tell me who it is? And what his reason might be?"

"The why's not my business. As to who, I really don't know. A man who claims he represents the United States government."

Arthur snorted. "Might I remind you, Mr. Slocum, that *I* am the chief representative of the United States government."

"Maybe," Slocum said.

He heard a sudden splashing behind him and turned to see Bellows fording the river on his scruffy paint, leading the bay and the pack mule. He didn't look to be in any hurry, so Slocum figured things were all right. Bellows brought the paint up out of the river, crossed the grassy bank to their little campsite, and swung down out of the saddle.

"Glad to see you," Bellows said. "I been following the river on the way down, and from the looks of that rough water I was afraid you maybe hadn't made it."

"We made it," Slocum said. "Barely. Raft busted up about an hour upstream, and we had to walk the rest of the way. How did it go?"

"Like a charm," Bellows said. "I cut trail north for almost four hours, then doubled back. Stuck to creeks and streams as much as I could. I was about two miles west of the camp when I passed it coming down, but there didn't look to be any fuss. I figure they wrote it off to them drunks just shooting at something that wasn't there. Likely they don't even know Mr. Arthur here is missing yet." He hunkered down beside Slocum and held his hands out to the fire. "The colonel not here yet?"

"No sign of him," Slocum said.

Arthur perked up at the mention of a colonel. "Are you saying the army is behind this?"

Bellows seemed a little surprised. "Our man here still in the dark?"

"Your friend has been less than forthcoming," Arthur told him. "Perhaps you might be a little more informative."

Bellows grinned. "Well, Mr. President, there's some who don't believe you belong in the office you hold."

"Who? And for what reason?"

Bellows glanced at Slocum. "Why not tell him? He'll find it out soon enough. They tell me, Mr. President, that you got where you are because the real president got himself shot. Assassinated. Garfield, I believe his name was. Evidently there's people back in Washington, powerful people, who think you were behind the shooting. As a way of getting yourself into the White House."

Arthur looked as if he thought he hadn't heard

right. His eyebrows went up, and he gazed off across the river as if he might find in the morning air some explanation for human folly. "And you believe them?"

"Not my job to believe them," Bellows said. "We was hired to get you out here, where these people could have a little talk with you. What happens then's not our business."

"When are these people due to arrive? This colonel you mentioned?"

"Any time now," Slocum said.

Arthur stared into the fire, where the salt pork he'd flung there was slowly roasting. "I suppose it would do me no good to try to convince you I had nothing to do with the assassination of President Garfield."

"Like he just got through saying," Slocum said, "that's not our business."

He left the fire, unfastened a pannier on the pack mule, and dug around in it until he found his boots and a change of clothes. Sleeping in that buffalo robe had smeared grease all over what he was wearing. He hoped the colonel would show up soon so he could get Arthur out of his sight. He was sick of this whole business. The fresh clothes made him feel a bit better. He strapped his gunbelt on, got a coffee pot and a couple of tin cups from the packsaddle, and returned to the fire. Arthur was still gazing into the glowing coals, brooding.

The sight of the coffee pot brought a little life to Arthur's face. "You didn't happen to bring something decent to eat with you?" he asked Bellows.

"Got some hardtack and bacon," Bellows said. "Dried beef too. Likely that's not what a man like you would call decent. There's plenty of game around here, but I ain't about to kill something for you. Never can tell who might be within earshot.''

''Well, if one of you would be so kind as to cut me a willow pole, I might try catching myself a decent breakfast.'' Arthur dropped the buffalo robe and stood up, checking the pockets of his fisherman's vest. ''If I'm going to have to wait, I might as well be active. You're welcome to share what I catch.''

Slocum exchanged a look with Bellows and shrugged. ''Why not?'' He unsheathed his knife and tossed it to Arthur. ''Here. You can cut your own willow pole.''

Arthur hefted the big Bowie, but if it gave him any ideas, the sight of the Colt strapped to Slocum's hip made him change his mind. Slocum watched him shamble off to the river's edge and search through some willows growing there, hunting a pole the right size.

''What do you think?'' he said to Bellows.

''About what?''

''About what he said. You think he had anything to do with it?''

''Can't tell. Can't ever tell with a man like that. Putting a good face on a lie is a politician's trade. Anyway, it don't make no difference. We done what we're being paid to do. That's all that counts.''

''Maybe to you. It's not all that counts to me. I never did trust that colonel. I'd hate to think I'd put myself on the wrong side of this thing.''

''In a thing like this, the right side's the side that wins. And we got no say in that. If the colonel and his people are wrong, likely they'll find it out. We're just hired hands.''

''Well, I've always been particular who I hired out to.''

Arthur had cut and trimmed his pole and was standing at the river's edge now, tying a line to the end of it, the knife stuck down in his belt. Slocum took the coffee pot to the river, filled it with water, and went over to retrieve the knife. Arthur was intent on his work and didn't look at him.

''What are you going to use for bait?'' Slocum asked.

''One of these.''

Arthur took a length of leader from a vest pocket and fixed it to the end of the line. There was a small hook at the end of the leader, festooned with something like tiny feathers, but it didn't look like any bait Slocum had ever seen. When Arthur had the line rigged up, he took a step or two back and whipped the pole over his head, slinging the line out over the water, where the little feathered hook landed lightly, floating on the surface.

''I haven't fished with a willow pole since I was a boy,'' he said.

''You seem pretty unconcerned for a man in your predicament.''

Arthur watched the feathered dot float downstream, giving an occasional tug on the line. ''You did say that my predicament, as you call it, is none of your affair; that you were just the agents hired to get me here. The best I can do is wait and see who these people are and what they want from me.''

''What they want, according to the colonel, is a confession.''

Arthur snorted. "A confession! Whether or not you believe it, Mr. Slocum, or whether or not you care, the assassination of President Garfield was the work of a madman. I had nothing to do with it. Do you even know the man's name?"

"The assassin? No, I don't."

"Then you don't know that he was already tried, convicted, and hanged. His name was Charles Guiteau. It's true he considered himself part of my wing of the party and tried to work his way into a position of influence. He attached himself to the New York headquarters during the campaign, did some writing of campaign leaflets, addressed a few rallies. After the election, he even met briefly with President Garfield. And it is true that by putting me in the White House he believed he was, in his words, 'saving the party.' But his true belief was that he was meant to save the world. Since you seem woefully ill-informed about the whole affair, it's safe to assume you did not read the accounts of the trial. Guiteau shouted at the witnesses, questioned prospective jurors on biblical doctrine, and often claimed to speak for the Almighty Himself. When I refused to rescind the death sentence, he claimed I was possessed by the devil. The man was obviously not mentally sound, Mr. Slocum."

Arthur abruptly yanked back on his pole, and from the river came the wild thrashing of the fish he'd hooked. The fish leaped from the water as Arthur worked it back and forth across the pool; he angled the pole up to where he could get a hold on the line and began pulling it in hand over hand. When he had the fish up on the bank, Slocum saw that it was a good-sized trout, gaping and flopping in the grass.

Arthur removed the fish from the hook, slipped a length of cord through one of its gills, and slung it from his belt, a short stick knotted through the end of the cord holding the still wriggling fish in place. "No, Mr. Slocum, Charles Guiteau was a madman. At one point in his life, during the Civil War years, while living in a utopian community in upstate New York, he even claimed he was destined to become ruler of the world." Arthur checked the hook, then whipped the line out over the river again. "Even if I were so foolish as to believe I could become President by hiring the assassination of my predecessor, do you really believe I would have chosen such an unstable man to do the deed?"

Slocum shrugged. He felt as if he were being lectured by a schoolmaster, and he didn't think Arthur really expected an answer.

"It was our misfortune," Arthur said, "that Charles Guiteau believed he was meant for great things and thought he would be granted a patronage job for his efforts on behalf of the campaign. When President Garfield denied his request, he sought revenge like the madman he was. That is one of the evils of the system I have been endeavoring to change: the handing out of civil service jobs through patronage. I am trying to initiate civil service reform, whereby such jobs will be attained through examinations of merit and capability and will be held by right of tenure. Now they are parceled out to cronies of each new administration, and it was Guiteau's unsuccessful effort to acquire such a job that led him to assassinate President Garfield.

"All that is well known. So you can believe that these people who have hired you, whoever they are, have evil designs of their own. They wish to pressure me into something. It is even possible they have concocted some false evidence to implicate me in the assassination, which they will try to hold over my head—isolated out here, away from friends and family—until I agree to go along."

Slocum wasn't sure he understood all that about patronage and reform, but he had the uneasy feeling that the part about somebody using this to pressure Arthur just might be true. He had never trusted the colonel, and just as he usually found he had good cause when he mistrusted a man, he was usually right when he found himself trusting one too. He often felt he could judge a man not so much by what the man said as by the way he said it and the way he handled himself, and he was beginning to believe Arthur was telling the truth. He didn't like the feeling that gave him.

When Arthur had caught five trout, he borrowed Slocum's knife again, gutted and cleaned the fish, and cut some more willow poles, with which he rigged up a spit over the fire. "I'm not so helpless in this wilderness as you might think," he said. "I've been a fisherman for more than forty years, and I know how to make myself something to eat." He nodded toward the salt pork turning black in the fire. "Better than that, at any rate."

Slocum had to admit that the trout, roasted with a little salt from the ration kits, was a hell of a lot better than salt pork and hardtack. He had the coffee pot on the fire, and the good smell of coffee was beginning to fill the air. He caught Arthur watching him as he ate. Slocum figured the man was going to make a pitch soon, try to get them to let him go, and he didn't know how he was going to deal with it. There was Bellows to think of, and Bellows had no reason to agree. Likely they were in too deep now, anyway. You didn't abduct the President and get away with it, even if you changed your mind later and set the man free. And the colonel could show up with his people any time now; from the look of the sun on that grassy clearing across the river, it was getting on toward eight in the morning. Arthur had to have been missed by now; camp usually served breakfast at six-thirty, and that cavalry escort was likely in a panic. They just might decide to send out search parties in all directions, despite the trail Bellows had laid going north.

Arthur finished his fish and wiped his hands on his trouser legs. "Tell me, Mr. Slocum, if you hadn't believed I was guilty of what you'd been told, would you have agreed to this job, snatching me out of camp and bringing me here?"

"I had no reason to believe otherwise," Slocum said.

"That wasn't my question."

Slocum knew Bellows wouldn't like it, but he figured he owed Arthur the truth. "Probably not."

Arthur nodded, as if that confirmed something he had suspected. "And if I convinced you I was not guilty, would you return me to my camp? If I could promise you would not be pursued or prosecuted?"

"Hold it a minute," Bellows said. "I'm in this thing too, you know."

"I doubt you could prove it, anyway," Slocum said. "And surely not in the time you have. That colonel should be here any minute. Should have been here already. I got to turn you over to him. That's what I contracted for.''

Arthur was regarding him with keen eyes. ''Somehow, Mr. Slocum, I believe you are an honest man.''

Slocum smiled. ''There's been some evidence in the past to dispute that.''

''Nonetheless,'' Arthur said, ''I believe I am a good judge of character, and I believe you are an honest man. And I think you know now that whoever hired you is up to no good. I believe you know I am an honest man too.''

''Don't make no difference now,'' Bellows said. ''Look yonder. Our man's finally arrived.''

Arthur turned abruptly to see what Bellows was pointing at: riders coming at a trot over the grassy hillock across the river, at least a dozen blue-uniformed troopers, with the man who called himself Colonel Smith out in the lead. When the little group reined up and fanned out in a line along the crest of the hill, Slocum saw that one of them was leading a riderless horse. Their rifles were still in the saddle boots, but they had to be an intimidating sight to Arthur.

Arthur had risen to his feet, watching as the colonel walked his horse a little ways forward of the rest and signaled with a hand, beckoning them across.

''The army,'' he said. ''If I hadn't seen it, I wouldn't have believed it.''

''Well, you've seen it,'' Bellows said. ''You better believe it.'' He picked the coffee pot out of the coals, poured the coffee over the flames, and started kicking the fire out.

Slocum felt Arthur's eyes on him. There was no expression on the man's face, just that curious gaze, as if to see how Slocum was taking this now. Pretty calm for a man in his position, but he had to know it was too late for talking. Even if he wanted to, Slocum couldn't help the man now. Two men against a dozen troopers was bad odds, even if Bellows was of a mind to go along. And maybe Bellows was right; maybe a man like Arthur, a politician, could tell a lie as good as some men told the truth. Maybe Arthur was as guilty as the colonel said he was. In any case, there was nothing Slocum could do about it now.

He brought the horses over to the fire and handed the bay's reins to Arthur. "You ride the bay. Might be a little tricky fording that river without a saddle, and you got no shoes on. I'll ride the mule till we're across."

"Very kind of you," Arthur said, and there was a hint of angry irony in his voice. "I see they've brought me a mount, but I'm obliged for the temporary use of yours." He declined assistance, stuck one bare foot in the stirrup, and hauled himself into the saddle.

Bellows had stuck the coffee pot and the cups back in the packsaddle and closed it up tight again. Slocum took the mule from him and hoisted himself up on its withers.

"All right," he said. "Let's get this thing over with."

16

Bellows led the way on his paint, Arthur in the middle, Slocum bringing up the rear on the mule. Bellows angled down along the bank to the downstream side of the pool, where the water was shallower, and they splashed across, Arthur jolting in the saddle and clinging to the horn, his feet bare and white in the stirrups. Once they were across, Slocum kicked the mule up alongside the others, and they trotted up the slope, reining to a halt where the colonel waited.

The colonel nodded to Slocum, that faint trace of amusement at the corners of his mouth. He glanced at Arthur and touched a hand to his hat. "Good morning, Mr. President."

"Do I know you?" Arthur asked.

"We have met," the colonel said. "I doubt you'd remember it. You were introduced to a lot of people that day. But I have some friends you know very well."

"I gathered that," Arthur said dryly.

Slocum was scanning the troopers who were with the colonel. He recognized Captain Williams, but Williams showed no sign of return recognition. They were all officers, about half of them captains or majors, the rest lieutenants. Whoever was running this show didn't trust it to remain secret if enlisted men were involved. About half of this bunch looked like political types from back East, officers used to riding a desk chair, not men seasoned in the Indian campaigns out here. Those who bore the marks of frontier experience had a similar look, though: that flushed look of ambition reaching higher than its grasp. They met his eyes with a kind of arrogant challenge, but he figured that was a cover. Knowing what an army officer's training bred into him, he couldn't imagine any of these men not feeling embarrassment at the sight of their President, knowing what they'd done and what they were planning to do next.

Whatever that was.

"Well, we delivered your package," Bellows said. "Seems you got something to deliver to us."

"I'm not in the habit of carrying fifty thousand dollars around in my saddlebags," the colonel said. "We'll split up here and take the President on with us. I think you'll agree it's best if you're cut out of it at this point. Captain Williams will escort you to the man who's acting as paymaster of this operation."

"And how far away would this paymaster be?" Bellows inquired.

"About a two-hour ride, south along the river. That'll take you away from the President's camp and give you a start on clearing out of the country. I assume that's what you have in mind. It's certainly what I'd recommend."

"And what happens to Arthur?" Slocum asked.

The colonel gave him all the force of those hard eyes, the faint smile still visible. "That will not be your affair, will it?" Without turning around, he waved up the man who was leading the riderless horse. "Mr. President, will you change mounts, please? I expect these men want to be on their way."

Arthur gave Slocum a long look: not hostile, not apprehensive, just a look that said he wanted Slocum to appreciate what he'd got himself involved in and what he had done. Then he dismounted from the bay and swung up on the cavalry mount. Slocum switched from the mule to the bay, tying the lead onto a saddlestring at the rear. When the switch was made, the colonel reined his horse around and nodded down the far side of the hill.

"You go first, Mr. President. We'll follow."

Slocum watched them go, five or six of the other officers immediately closing up around Arthur, the colonel trailing along behind. For the first time now he saw that there were other men waiting down at the bottom of the hill, about a hundred yards away, at the edge of a stand of trees running northwest up along what was likely a creek—more officers, standing by their mounts. It was too far away to tell for sure, but one of them looked to be wearing the shoulder straps of a general. The insignia on the straps was silver, which meant he had to be a lieutenant-colonel or above, but a lieutenant-colonel had only two silver leaves, and unless Slocum wasn't seeing right, this man had five of something. And if there were five, they had to be stars. One of the bunch was an Indian, likely a scout, too far away to make out which tribe. Maybe a Sioux; there were some Sioux scouts in the army, though it had been just seven years since the Sioux had killed Custer at the Little Bighorn.

"We'd better get started," Captain Williams said. "Troop G has had about three hours now, once they missed the President at breakfast. They should have followed the trail you left to lead them off north, but they may have sent some troops south too. The sooner we get away, the better."

Slocum saw that six of the officers had stayed— one captain besides Williams, and four lieutenants. He didn't like the looks of that. It didn't take six pencil-pushing officers to escort two experienced men on a short ride down a riverbank. He caught Bellows's eye and saw that Bellows had noted it too.

"You're the boss," he said. "Let's go find this paymaster of yours."

They were out of sight of the colonel's bunch in minutes, riding down along the west bank of the Snake. At first the terrain was treeless and grassy; then they crossed the mouth of that creek along which the others had been waiting, and a little timbered ridge rose up on the right, leaving a clear stretch of ground about thirty yards wide between the trees and the sharp drop to the river on the left. Two of the lieutenants had taken the lead, the second captain was riding along the edge of the timber on the right, and Williams and the other two lieutenants were bringing up the rear. Slocum began to get the uncomfortable feeling that he was boxed in.

After a few minutes, Bellows brought his paint up close alongside Slocum's bay. Under his breath, he said, "Is it just my imagination, or do these boys look a little unfriendly?"

"I noticed that," Slocum said. "*Very* unfriendly. Definitely not your imagination."

"Maybe you also noticed we're a mite outnumbered. I'm trying to figure why we need six men to help us find our way to what they're calling their paymaster. With Arthur's party likely scouring the country for him, seems they'd need every man they got, if only to keep watch.''

"Maybe they figure these six have got something more important to do."

"I'm afraid you're right," Bellows said.

Slocum looked around to make sure none of the others was within earshot. The three at the rear were about thirty yards back, the two in front about the same distance ahead. Only the second captain was closer, riding parallel, but he wouldn't be able to hear them, talking as softly as they were.

"You ever hear about the king that buried the treasure?" Bellows said.

Slocum looked at him. "This have something to do with this little party we're going on, or are you just trying to take my mind off things?"

"Story I heard when I was a boy," Bellows said. "Rich king. Wanted to hide a treasure. Off somewhere like Persia, if I remember right, back in olden times. Took him a bunch of slaves out to pick a secret spot and had them bury the treasure. Only thing was, the slaves knew where he buried it. So he took them off a ways somewhere and brought up another bunch of slaves and had the second bunch kill the first. So nobody'd know where the treasure was buried. And then he had a third bunch of slaves kill the second, just to make sure."

"I never heard the story," Slocum said, "but I've got the uneasy feeling you just put your finger on what's going on here."

Bellows glanced across at the captain riding parallel along the foot of the ridge. "Slocum," he said, "I do believe we have been played for suckers."

"I told you I didn't trust that colonel."

"Yeah, and I wish now I'd listened to you. But fifty thousand dollars can make a man's hearing go bad awful fast. How much time do you figure we got?"

"Likely they want to get far enough south so there's no chance of Arthur's people hearing shots. We're pretty far downstream now. I figure maybe twenty minutes, half an hour. Your guess is as good as mine."

"How do you figure it'll come?"

Slocum glanced back at the three in the rear. "Williams'll trigger it off, I expect. Maybe that's why he's behind us. So we can't see the signal. But they won't do it strung out like they are now. Too much risk of hitting each other. You see them start changing formation, you better be ready to move fast."

"Well," Bellows said, "my mama told me to be a good boy. And look at what I went and got myself into."

Slocum's mind had come suddenly alert and alive, but nothing he could think of offered much hope. He couldn't see anything through the trees growing up the riverbank, but from the sound of the river, he could tell it was running through a deep gorge, the drop-off sharp and abrupt. They couldn't make a run for it in that direction. The ridge on the right was steep from the very start, and that second captain was in the way, but the timber up there was dense enough to provide cover if they could get into it.

"Breaking right up the ridge is the only hope we

got,'' he said. ''We'll have to ride over that captain, but if we do it now, fast, when they're not expecting it, we might have a chance.''

Bellows was watching the captain. ''Better cut that pack mule loose,'' he said. ''We don't want anything slowing us down.''

Slocum started to reach for the lead rope tied to his saddlestring. He didn't even have time to turn around before he heard the voice behind him: Captain Williams, and closer than he ought to be.

''Just hold it where you are,'' Williams said. ''This is as far as we go.''

Slocum reined to a halt, the skin between his shoulder blades prickling in anticipation of a bullet. He didn't turn his head, but he could see Bellows pulling up the paint beside him, poised and careful not to move too much. The two lieutenants in the lead circled their horses up into the trees along the base of the ridge, hauling their carbines out. He had to restrain an impulse to go for his Colt; they were too far away for accuracy with a pistol, and one fast move would only get him shot in the back. Play it one step at a time, he told himself; as long as you're alive, there's always a chance.

Carefully, he edged the bay around until his back was to the river. Bellows did the same, putting his paint at an angle to the bay so they were both facing the ridge, but with a line of sight in each direction.

Williams had led the lieutenants with him up off the right of the trail and halted about twenty yards away, facing Slocum. The lieutenants had their carbines up, pointing right at him. The other captain had backed his horse into the trees to the left of them, and from the corner of his eye Slocum could see the two in the lead walking their horses back until they were about twenty yards to the left of the captain. He was caught in a box, with four carbines trained on him. Neither of the captains had a gun out; evidently this little execution was going to be the lieutenants' work.

"I take it this is where we get paid off," Slocum said.

"You can call it that," Williams said.

Slocum eyed the carbines. It was a dirty way to die: shot down cold by a bunch of bluebellies. He had spent his youth fighting bluebellies, and now the old word came back, and with it that scarcely remembered surge of Rebel rage. Maybe it was a dirty way to die, but he could take at least one of them with him. That captain calling himself Williams, for instance.

"I should have known people planning a thing like this would pay it off with a bullet," he said.

"You got last words coming, I guess," Williams said. "You might as well get 'em out."

Slocum judged the distance between them. A chance for one shot maybe before he was cut down. Right in the captain's gut. "The only words I got are for your bosses. I figure you're too dumb to see what you're doing. Start this, and you'll be killing your own before too long. We'll have another real nice little civil war."

"I remember you didn't do too well in the last one," Williams said. "And, anyway, I'm just following my orders, like I was trained to do."

"Well, I never liked following orders," Bellows said. "Especially yours."

He took his hat off and hung it on his saddle horn.

What came next happened so fast Slocum lost most of it in a blur of gunfire, the squealing of horses, and a high-pitched *yip-yip-yip* coming from the trees. He heard a quick *thuck, thuck, thuck,* and an arrow suddenly sprouted out of Williams's throat. Bellows was diving off the paint, whooping, hitting the ground and rolling. A carbine fired somewhere on Slocum's left, the bullet crackling past his ear, but he was already following Bellows's lead.

He hit the ground with his Colt out, the spooked bay blocking his line of sight. He dodged the pack mule and grabbed the bay's stirrup, keeping it between him and the ridge. A quick glance under its belly showed him Williams dead on the ground and one of the lieutenants sagging in the saddle with an arrow in his back. The other had fallen from his mount, his boot caught in the stirrup, and he was being dragged in a wide circle as the panicked horse tried to get away.

The bay started to bolt. Slocum seized the reins in time to see an Indian tackle the second captain from a tree, knocking him off his horse in a wild roll down the slope, a gleaming knife in an upraised hand. Another shot came from the left, and he ducked that way. Bellows was up on one knee, firing at a cavalry mount trotting wild-eyed toward them, one of the other lieutenants clinging to its neck, the shaft of an arrow sticking up between his shoulder blades. His partner had wheeled his mount and was fleeing down the riverbank at a gallop. Now an Indian on a calico pony broke out of the trees behind him, whooping, black hair flying, kicking his pony in the ribs. Without slackening pace, the Indian leaned along the pony's neck holding a rifle and brought the lieutenant down with one shot.

Slocum was suddenly aware of the bay shying and jerking at the reins, the pack mule lunging at the end of its lead rope. Still in something of a daze, he hunted for a target, but there was nothing left to shoot at.

The Indian in the trees had slit the captain's throat and now rose spraddle-legged above him, clad in buckskin leggings and a red shirt, a gun belt buckled around his waist, his knife still dripping blood. Bellows had shot the wounded lieutenant out of the saddle; he leaped to seize the wild-eyed horse by its bridle. The horse dragged him along the ground until he had it stopped, and now two more Indians rode down out of the trees to pursue the others, dodging and turning to cut them off, leaning out to grab the trailing reins.

Still dazed, Slocum holstered his Colt. The Indian on the calico pony had ridden down the horse of the man he'd killed and was leading it back toward them. Slocum was streaming with sweat. He wiped a sleeve across his face.

Bellows looked a little pale, and his hands were shaking as he wrapped the cavalry mount's reins around the paint's saddle horn. "I'm getting too old for this kind of thing," he said. "You all right?"

"Far as I can tell." Slocum was feeling a little shaky. He fumbled makings from his pocket and started clumsily rolling a smoke. "Never got off a shot. I guess I owe you one."

"You don't owe me a thing," Bellows said. "That was my hide at stake just then too."

The Indian with the knife led his pony down out

of the trees, leaped on its back, and rode down to join the others crowding up around Bellows. There were four of them, all wearing breechclouts, knee-high moccasins, and thigh-length red shirts, cartridge belts strapped around their waists. They had rifles, but each of them had a bow slung over his neck.

"I kind of figured going into this wasn't safe without some backup," Bellows said, "so I had Jim Fisher send word we might need a little help. This here is Running Wolf," he said, nodding to the Indian who had tackled the captain off his horse. "Two-Hat, Walking Bear, and Little Fox. Best Indian scouts the army ever had. They been drifting along behind us for days."

The Indians grinned, eyes still glittering with the fierce joy of battle. Running Wolf had a gold ring in one ear and two lengths of braid dangling down below his collarbone. The rest of his hair hung loose and greasy. The other three wore their hair the same way, but Running Wolf had the lower third of his braids encased in wolf's pelt, fur side out. Two-Hat wore a wide-brimmed white man's hat, which was perhaps where he'd got his name, and they all had several strings of beads draped around their necks.

"Wish I'd known that," Slocum said. "I'd have breathed a lot easier just then."

"Would have told you," Bellows said, "but I didn't want 'em tied to this if I could help it. They ain't supposed to be off the reservation. I had my suspicions about the colonel too. Especially when it came to getting paid off. Didn't know where we might be when trouble hit, so I told the boys here not to use their guns unless there was already shooting going on.'' He took out a plug of tobacco and bit off a chew. ''What you figure we ought to do now?''

Slocum had finally got his cigarette built; he touched a match to it, grateful for the smoke. ''We've got to get out of what we put ourselves into. We've already killed six of the colonel's men, and when they find that out, you can bet his people will hunt us down. They can't afford to let us live. And we already put Arthur against us. We're caught in the middle, and we got to get somebody on our side. Arthur's our only chance. We got to get him back from the colonel.''

Bellows glanced back upstream. ''I don't fancy heading back in that direction. No telling where Arthur's escort is. They may have sent search parties this way, like that Captain Williams said. Could be they heard that gunfire.''

''We got to risk it,'' Slocum said. ''We got to buy ourselves some insurance. Otherwise we'll have people hunting us for the rest of our days. If we rescue Arthur, he might agree to call things square.''

''Guess that's our best bet—or the only one. But we better do it fast. The colonel will be wondering what happened to his firing squad.'' He turned to the Indians. ''How about it, boys? You know what we're up against. We fail at this, we'll likely get ourselves hanged. You game?''

Running Wolf grinned. ''Long time ago, Running Wolf kill many pony soldiers. Maybe time kill many pony soldiers again, huh?''

''Only when I tell you to, you crazy Indian,'' Bellows said. ''We ain't on the warpath here. We're just trying to get the big Washington chief back from the colonel and save our hides.''

"We get him back, you bet," Two-Hat said. "Colonel's pony soldiers not warriors. Too much fat in face. You say go, we catch 'em up plenty quick."

Bellows looked around at the bodies strewn on the ground—six cavalrymen killed in a matter of seconds. "What do we do with these fellas? Can't leave 'em here like this."

"Let's strip the bodies," Slocum said. "And we'll take their mounts. No telling what the situation will be when we find the colonel, but I got an idea. If things go right, those uniforms can come in handy."

Hurriedly, they stripped the bodies, and Slocum stashed the uniforms and boots in the packsaddle on the mule. Running Wolf and the other Indians dragged the corpses to the edge of the deep gorge and dumped them into the fast-running river below. When Bellows had the cavalry mounts rigged up on a lead rope, Slocum swung back up on the bay.

"Let's make it fast," he said, "but keep your eyes and ears open. We don't want to run up on anybody unexpected."

17

Riding fast, they covered the ground back to where they'd turned Arthur over to the colonel in half the time it had taken with Williams and his detail on the way down. Running Wolf was in the lead, scanning the terrain ahead, the other Indians bunched up close behind him. Slocum came next, leading the mule, and Bellows followed with the cavalry mounts. Torn between the need for speed and the need for caution, Slocum had to restrain an urge to travel at a flat-out gallop. It would do them no good to catch up to the colonel's party if Arthur's escort beat them to it— or, worse, if something had already happened to Arthur.

He remembered that Indian scout he'd seen waiting with the colonel's bunch down by the creek. A Sioux, he'd thought. The Sioux had been known to take a great deal of pleasure in torturing a prisoner. He wondered if the colonel would resort to that. They wanted a confession, and a lot of confessions had been wrung out of men that way. And once you'd taken the step the colonel and his people had—seizing the President himself, putting themselves all in danger of being hanged if they didn't get what they wanted—why, a little torture wouldn't seem too far out of line. If they found themselves not getting their confession, it might even seem the next logical, necessary step.

Running Wolf slowed when they reached the creek running down from the northwest. They walked the horses up to where it emptied into the river, the Indians watching the ground. Nothing but the hoofprints they and Williams's detail had left coming downriver. Wherever the colonel's bunch was, they hadn't come this way. They rode on across the creek, slowing again as they neared the rendezvous point. Running Wolf raised a hand to halt them when they came in sight of last night's campfire.

Slocum held the bay quiet and listened. All he could hear was the river's steady rush. The only tracks he could see were those they'd left after they had forded the river.

"You wait," Running Wolf said, and kicked his pony up the little hill the colonel had come across that morning. He slid to the ground about halfway up and dropped to his belly, wriggling up through the grass. Only the waving of the grass showed where he was, and soon even that was invisible.

He reappeared about five minutes later, bellying down the hill until he was far enough below the crest to get to his feet. He trotted back down the slope, leading his pony by the reins.

"See nobody now," he said. "Before, they by little river, but no tracks lead away. I think maybe go into trees. Maybe go up little river."

"That's the way I'd go if I was them," Bellows said. "Put that ridge between me and Arthur's people, head up into those mountains to the northwest. Could be they got somebody waiting up there, somebody they're taking Arthur to. Let's go scout that place where we saw them last.''

Running Wolf launched himself onto his pony and they rode back downstream, crossed the little creek, and cut northwest through the trees along its bank. The trees here were aspen, growing pretty far apart. The ground was as flat as a floor, covered with tall grass a bright green in the dappled sunlight, with only the occasional bone-white skeleton of a downed tree to mar the effect. Slocum hoped the timber was denser farther upstream; a man could see a long way through these aspen, and he was counting on getting close without being spotted.

About a hundred yards upstream they found the spot where the colonel's bunch had crossed the creek. Running Wolf called a halt and got down to examine the hoofprints.

''Twelve hoss,'' he said. ''Go upstream. One hoss, he wear no iron shoes. Indian pony. Sioux, I think, maybe.''

''One Indian,'' Bellows said. ''One horse for Arthur. Means there's ten of the colonel's people. How fast are they moving?''

Running Wolf led his pony a little ways upstream. ''They go fast, but not running. Fast trot, I bet you.''

''We better put these cayuses to a lope, then,'' Bellows said. ''Running Wolf, you get out ahead a ways so's you can hear something besides us.''

They rode on upstream, Running Wolf loping about fifty yards ahead, head down, watching the trail. Across the creek, above a rise of treeless ground, Slocum could see an extension of that ridge back at the river. It was almost flat on top, heavily timbered, and seemed to parallel the creek, the grassy slopes running down from it furrowed with little ravines likely cut by spring runoff. If he'd been alone, he would have picked a route along that ridge, where a man could spot somebody down in this timber without being seen himself. But then they'd have the problem of coming down that treeless slope unnoticed. And he trusted Bellows and his scouts; he was a fair woodsman himself, but he couldn't cut trail like an Indian.

After about two miles, Running Wolf slowed his pony to a trot, leaning down to get a closer look at the trail. When they came up even with him, he said, "Hoss go slow now. Steady walk, like maybe have long ride ahead."

Bellows was leaning down to scan the tracks. "Likely they figure they've put enough ground behind them to be safe. Either that, or they're going slow to let Williams and his firing squad catch up."

"We better keep it at a trot," Slocum said. "You figure Running Wolf'll know when we're getting close?"

"He'll know. Running Wolf can track prey like his namesake. He could sneak up and snatch your hair before you heard him coming."

They rode on at a trot, Running Wolf moving out ahead again. The ground had begun to climb a little, and Slocum was glad to see the aspen gradually giving way to lodgepole pine, most of it no bigger around than his arm but dense enough to provide some cover. He figured it was nearly noon by the sun, and that meant Troop G had had over six hours to do some tracking of their own. And they had Indian scouts with them too. Even if they followed

Bellows's trail to its end, once it petered out they would figure it had been set on purpose to lead them off north. The logical thing then would be to turn back south. All they'd have to do would be to follow the river downstream until they picked up the real trail, and they could do that practically at a run. They could be coming up the creek behind him right now. He didn't like the feeling that gave him.

About a mile farther on, his pony still at a trot, Running Wolf slid down off its back and began running along in front of it, scanning the ground, the reins in his hand. When the rest of them caught up with him, he was down on one knee, probing at a hoofprint with one finger.

Two-Hat slipped down to join him; he picked at some horse droppings with a twig and glanced at Running Wolf. "Close," he said.

Running Wolf nodded, looking off up the trail. He got to his feet and started unbuckling his gun belt. Stripped to the waist, he handed the shirt and gun belt and the pony's reins to Two-Hat.

"You walk hoss now," he said to Bellows. "Keep quiet like sleep. Running Wolf go have look-see."

Clad in his breechclout and moccasins, carrying only a knife for a weapon, he trotted off to the right of the trail. In an instant he had faded into the brush along the bank.

They started on at a walk. Two-Hat moved out in front now, leading Running Wolf's pony. Slocum kept his ears cocked, listening for movement up ahead, but all he could hear was the sound of his own mount stepping delicately along through the pines, one of the other horses breaking wind, the sigh of a little breeze through the treetops.

The creek was obscured by thick brush, but those treeless slopes and the densely timbered bluff above them were still visible rising up to the north of it. The pines along the creek bank grew fairly close together, but the trunks were so slender that he could see a good fifty yards ahead, and there was no sign of movement up there. Still worrying about Arthur's escort, he turned to listen back along the way they had come, but the woods were quiet, not even the sound of a bird breaking the silence.

They had gone maybe a quarter of a mile when Two-Hat reined in and raised a hand to halt them. Slocum hadn't seen or heard anything, but they had barely pulled up when Running Wolf came trotting out of the trees on the right, his breechclout flapping between his knees. Likely he had trotted the whole way there and back, but he didn't look at all winded. He retrieved his pony from Two-Hat and led it back to Bellows.

"Ten pony soldier," he said. "Sioux scout break trail, rest all bunch up. Not far now." He grinned. "Nobody watch out. Everybody think safe. I think maybe we kill him now, huh?"

"What about Arthur?" Slocum said. "The big chief from Washington. Where they got him?"

"Keep hoss tight together," Running Wolf said. "Big chief ride in middle. Hands tied to saddle. Him hoss he lead by pony soldier."

Bellows gazed off upstream, ruminating. "Why don't we just track 'em till night? Wait till they bed down. We could sneak into camp and maybe get Arthur out without any fuss. These boys got a lot of practice doing things like that."

"We can't afford to wait," Slocum said. "Be

another eight or nine hours till nightfall. Arthur's troops could catch up to us before then. We got to get Arthur out of there and have time to talk a deal with him. And if Williams doesn't show up with his detail, they'll get suspicious. We have to take 'em now, while they think they're safe."

Bellows nodded reluctantly. "We're a mite outnumbered, though. How you figure on doing it?"

"They ought to be expecting Williams back about now. That's why I wanted the uniforms. There was six of them—there's six of us. We change into those uniforms and ride the cavalry mounts, we can maybe get almost up to them before they realize who we are. When they do, we should be close enough to charge right through them, kill as many as we can, and cut Arthur loose in the confusion."

Bellows looked around at his scouts, who had crowded up to listen. "What do you say, boys? Be a good trick if we can pull it off. Think you can pass for pony soldiers?"

Walking Bear hadn't said a word since the fight back at the river. Now he tilted his head up like maybe he was a little insulted. "Crow scout make fine pony soldier. We fool 'em, you bet. Steal Big Chief Atha like wind take smoke from fire."

Little Fox nodded and laughed as though the idea tickled his fancy, and Running Wolf had that glitter in his eyes again. Slocum breathed a little more easily. You could never tell how an Indian might take to putting on a dead man's clothes. They could carry around a bloody scalp without a thought of the head it had come from, but they had a lot of superstitions too. Sometimes getting too close to a dead man, and especially the dead man's effects, could put fear into a brave who'd think nothing of risking his hide in a fight.

It didn't seem to bother this bunch, though; they were already stripping off their shirts, laughing and gabbling in that language he didn't understand. He swung down off the bay and got the uniforms and boots from the packhorse.

Williams had worn about the same size he did; he stripped and put the captain's uniform on, feeling a little queasy himself about the blood caked around the collar from that arrow Williams had taken in the throat. His feet filled the boots about right too, but the Indians had more of a problem. There wasn't one of them big enough to match the uniforms available, and they weren't too happy about wearing boots, especially boots that didn't fit. He had to do some talking to get them out of their moccasins, and even then they put the uniform pants on directly over their breechclouts, tucking the rawhide flap up through the crotch. When they were all outfitted up, they jostled together like troopers at an inspection, grinning, shoulders back, chins tucked in, but they were a pretty sloppy-looking detail: coats too big, sleeves that hung down to their fingertips, baggy pants tucked into the cavalry boots.

"Better get them to stuff all that hair up under their hats," he told Bellows. "As a matter of fact, you better do the same. Too bad we ain't got time to shave off that beard. You don't look much like one of them shavetail lieutenants."

Bellows had put one of the lieutenants' uniforms on, and, except for the beard, he would pass. He was fingering a bloody hole where an arrow had passed through his shirt. "Sure hope that ain't an omen," he said.

Slocum brought the cavalry mounts up and loosed them from their lead rope. The carbines were back in the saddle boots, but rifles looked pretty much alike from a distance; he gave in on that and let the scouts carry their own. He had to shorten the stirrups for them, but they swung up like veterans, sitting proud and cocky in the saddle. He figured this was the first time they'd ever had uniforms on; a lot of army units formed their scouts into regular squads, uniforms and all, but Bellows had insisted he wanted his scouts to stay Indian.

Bellows was adjusting the stirrups on his own mount. "What'll we do with our horses?" he said. "Hate to leave them behind."

"We'll take them with us," Slocum said. "Williams wouldn't have left them out there. Riderless horses wandering around could make somebody suspicious. And he'd need them to prove to the colonel that he did the job. We'll have your scouts bring them along at the rear. I'll take the lead, you next, then the scouts. We'll want them in back of us. Even in those uniforms, a man wouldn't have to get too close to see they're Indians."

He transferred the panniers and the packsaddle from the mule to Two-Hat's calico pony; that would disguise its markings a little. They had more horses than Williams would have been bringing with him, and the calico was a little obvious, but he would just have to hope the colonel's bunch didn't look too closely too soon.

When he had the mule and the horses rigged up, tying their reins at intervals to a long lead rope, he gave the lead to Little Fox and mounted Williams's long-legged sorrel. ''We'll go single file so they can't get a good look till we're on them,'' he said. ''Stay at a trot till they see us, at least. You can carry your rifles out and across your pommels. That'll look natural enough. Let's get as close as we can before we jump them. At the first sign they've recognized us, fan out and come at them at a run and put a bullet through every one of them you can. Only make sure you don't hit Arthur. I'll worry about cutting him loose. The rest of you don't slow up unless you absolutely have to. Hit them hard and fast, bust through them, and keep right on going.''

When he was sure the scouts had understood, he wheeled the sorrel and started upstream through the pines.

18

Slocum kept the sorrel at a fast trot, watching the trees up ahead. Changing clothes and horses had taken maybe twenty minutes, at most a half an hour. He figured the colonel's bunch might have covered another two or three miles in that time. It wouldn't take long to catch them.

The army's McClellan saddle wasn't as comfortable as the one on his bay, but the sorrel had a nice, easy stride, and he found himself beginning to feel good. He knew what that was: that keyed-up state he always got into just before the shooting started, when the air on his face began to seem sweeter and the sky bluer and he became sharply aware of things like the green of the grass on the slopes beyond the creek, the smell of the pines they were passing through. There was an added element to it this time, and it surprised him: he was glad he'd been forced to switch sides, that the job now was to put Arthur back where the country said he belonged, where the man did belong if Slocum's instincts were right. Maybe he had more allegiance to his country than he had thought.

He was following a little trail now winding through the pines, a narrow path worn smooth by deer or by Indians. He looked back to check on the others.

Bellows was about ten yards back, followed by the Indians in single file—Running Wolf in the lead, Little Fox bringing up the rear with the spare horses and the mule. They all had their rifles out. Bellows gave him a grin and a wave. The scouts still didn't look much like cavalrymen. Never mind the dark faces; something about the way they sat a horse marked them as Indians. But, if things went right, with surprise on their side, it wouldn't matter.

He heard the colonel's bunch before he saw them. Voices carried a long way through this high mountain air when there was no other sound around. He couldn't make out what was being said, but he recognized Arthur's voice, and it sounded as though he were having a hot argument with somebody. Then he began to see them through the trees: bits of blue uniform, the rump of a horse passing casually out of sight beyond a tree trunk, the head of a rider ducking under a limb.

A quick glance over his shoulder told him that Bellows and the scouts had also sighted them. He urged the sorrel on at that fast, jolting trot, anxious to close up and get this started. He had his knife out and shielded down along his leg; he would trust the others to do the shooting. His aim was to get to Arthur and cut the man loose. Then he rounded a bend in the trail and saw the colonel's bunch barely forty yards ahead.

They had stopped to water their horses at a shallow brook crossing the trail. The Sioux scout was already across, his pony turned and facing Slocum's way. The others sat easy in the saddle while the horses drank in a line along the near bank. Arthur was in the middle of the line, the lead rope stretching from his mount to a saddle string of the horse on his left. Slocum kept the sorrel at that fast trot, and now he saw heads begin to turn back toward the sound.

The colonel glanced toward him and turned to say something to the man on his right, a man wearing the shoulder straps of a general. The general said something in reply, watching Slocum approach.

And then the Sioux shouted and kicked his pony off into the trees to the left of the trail.

The colonel wheeled his mount. For an instant he just stared; then he went to clawing at his holster flap. Slocum let out a Rebel yell and spurred the sorrel into a gallop.

Rifle fire erupted behind him, and he heard that wild *yip-yip-yip* coming up the sides as Bellows and the scouts fanned out into the trees. The colonel was waving his pistol in the air, shouting at his troops. The whole bunch plunged across the brook and scattered into the trees, only the man with Arthur in tow galloping full tilt on up the trail. Slocum ignored the rest of them and spurred the sorrel straight on.

The Sioux had pulled up just to the left of the trail, tracking Slocum with a rifle as he came on. Slocum ducked as the sorrel splattered across the brook. Then a shot from somewhere spilled the Sioux off his pony, and Slocum was past him, lashing the sorrel with the reins, pounding after Arthur.

The cavalryman was riding flat-out, bent over the pommel, not looking back. Arthur was clinging to the saddle he was tied to, ducking overhanging branches, flinching away from tree trunks banging at his knees as the horse zig zagged along the trail. Slocum looped the reins over the pommel and brought his

Colt out, but with Arthur between them he couldn't get a clear shot. Then the trail swung left and then right again, and the man in the front was in the clear, and Slocum put a bullet in his back.

The man came suddenly erect, arms flung up, and pitched left out of the saddle, but his spooked horse galloped on. Slocum holstered the colt and flicked the spurs in again, slowly gaining on it. He came up alongside Arthur, the horses bobbing head to head. He saw Arthur flick a frightened glance his way. Then he was up past the withers, the neck, the bobbing head, and he leaned out to seize the lead rope, bringing the knife around to sever it from the saddle string. He took two quick turns of the lead rope around his wrist and kicked the sorrel on, the cavalryman's mount beginning to slow, falling away to the rear.

The firing was still going on behind him, but he didn't look back; he was hoping they wouldn't risk hitting Arthur. He caught the flash of horses flickering through the woods on his left and saw Bellows ramming another magazine into his rifle and Running Wolf beyond him, kicking his horse in the ribs and firing over his shoulder at the same time.

The firing had suddenly begun to die away. Bellows slashed through the trees and came out onto the trail beside him, still at a gallop.

"They're pulling back!" he shouted.

Slocum glanced back past Arthur to see the trail empty behind him. "The colonel's regrouping. Doesn't want all his troops killed in the confusion. They'll be after us in a minute. Let's cross the creek and try to make it up that bluff. Try to reach the high ground before they get organized."

Bellows whooped and shouted something in Crow, and Slocum saw the Indians slashing through the woods toward them. None of them seemed even wounded, and Little Fox still had the spare mounts on his string. Slocum checked to see that Arthur was all right, then swerved the sorrel off into the trees to the right and crashed through the brush along the creek.

The creek was shallow; they were across it in an instant and starting up a narrow little ravine at a run. The timber grew halfway down it near the top, and Slocum was hoping they could reach that timber before the colonel got his troops sorted out.

The sorrel, blowing hard, its hide matted with sweat, was already starting to labor as the slope steepened. Slocum looked back to see Arthur clinging to the pommel, white-faced, concentrating on staying aboard. Bellows had his head turned to watch the rear, where the Indians were kicking their horses on, long hair flying from under their cavalry hats.

There was still a good thirty yards to go when the first shot came from the treeline along the creek. The sorrel squealed and stumbled and started to go down.

Slocum vaulted from the saddle, the lead rope still wrapped around his wrist, and tried to yank the faltering sorrel up the side of the ravine and out of the way. He was not fast enough. Arthur's mount ran up on it and shied to the right; one hoof glanced off a rock and it staggered and almost fell, but Bellows was there to grab the lead rope, his horse not even breaking stride, lunging on up the slope with Arthur in tow. Firing had broken out all along the treeline, and Slocum could hear lead whining through the air.

The sorrel was foundering, blood spouting from a hole in its lungs. He shot it in the head and dropped down behind it, dragging the carbine out of the saddle boot. He heard another squeal and saw Running Wolf was already dodging toward Walking Bear's horse, grabbing its bridle and running alongside it, keeping it between him and the shots coming from below. Slocum emptied the carbine's magazine at the treeline as fast as he could work the lever, and then Walking Bear's horse passed him, and there was only Little Fox, twenty yards back, slowed up by that string of spare mounts. Now Slocum saw the mule go down, its reins breaking loose as it fell. Then Little Fox was lunging up past him, and he ducked under the lead rope to seize the mane of the next horse back, running along beside it until the whole bunch had struggled up into the trees choking the mouth of the ravine.

The ground rose almost straight up here, seven or eight feet to the top of the bluff. The horses were shying and milling as Bellows kicked his own up the steep slope, lashing it with the reins to drive it on. It lunged and staggered and slid back and lunged again, and then it was over the top, hauling Arthur's mount up with it. The Indians fought their way up, Walking Bear first, Running Wolf holding on to the horse's tail; Slocum clambered up after Little Fox and turned to seize the lead rope, pulling the spare horses up behind him.

The Indians leaped from their mounts and sprawled along the rim of the bluff, already returning fire from behind the shelter of tree trunks. Slocum led Arthur's mount at a trot back into the trees, out of the line of fire. He cut the ropes holding Arthur to the saddle and helped the man to the ground, where he sat trying to get his wind and his senses back, blowing as hard as any of the horses. Bellows had tethered the other horses back out of the way and was crawling up toward the tree behind which Running Wolf was sheltering, dragging his rifle. The firing was sporadic now, just enough to keep those troopers pinned in the trees.

Arthur was rubbing the circulation back into his wrists, white in the face and breathing hard. His hands were shaking.

"You all right?" Slocum said.

"I'm all right," Arthur said. "Just shaken up." He took a deep breath, and a sudden shudder ran through him as though he'd just come in out of the cold. That seemed to calm him down some. "Shouldn't we be moving? Won't they be after us?"

"They won't come up a treeless slope into fire from high ground. They'll circle around and try coming up this ridge another way. We got a little time. You want to tell me who they are? What they wanted from you?"

"We didn't discuss the particulars. There was someone else I was supposed to meet, somewhere over these mountains. And talk of evidence linking me to Garfield's assassination. Cooked-up evidence."

"Who's the next man in line for the job if you're forced out of office?"

"That wasn't the plan. Your friends down there were quite willing to have me remain as President. So long as they had that false evidence to hold over me, they believed I'd have to pursue the policies they wanted. A shadow government, with me as the figurehead." He rubbed his hands across his face, still not recovered from the scare. "And what about you? I thought you were on the other side. Who are these . . . these Indians? And why are you in uniform?"

"The Indians are Bellows's scouts. They used to work for him in the army. And let's just say I changed my mind. Got to thinking about that talk we had this morning. Decided I'd put myself on the wrong side of this thing. We figured wearing uniforms we could get in and cut you loose before the colonel realized who we were." He decided not to mention the killing of Williams's detail; let Arthur think the uniforms had come from the same place the scouts had.

"What happens now?" Arthur said.

"I figured to return you to camp—if we can get away from the colonel's bunch down there."

"That might be a little risky for you."

"We didn't plan on going back ourselves. But we can get you close enough so you can go in on your own. Troop G may even be heading this way by now. As for what happens to us, that's more or less up to you. I seem to remember you guaranteeing us no pursuit and no prosecution if we turned you back over to your own people."

Firing suddenly broke out along the rim of the bluff again. "They're heading west up the creek!" Bellows shouted. "Planning to circle back along this ridge. They know we can't go east—might run into Troop G."

Slocum ran in a crouch back to the edge of the trees and dropped down beside Bellows. He was just in time to catch a glimpse of blue flashing through the woods along the far side of the creek below—the colonel's bunch, heading west, Bellows had said. "Hold your fire," he said. "Don't waste ammunition on targets you can't see. How many they got left?"

"Seven or eight," Bellows said. "I shot the Sioux and a couple of horses, so some of them may be riding double. Things happened too fast to count, but they got at least seven."

Arthur had crawled up beside them, peering down the hillside. Slocum looked around at the ridge; it was about the narrowest ridge he'd ever seen, and it sloped away in every direction. He figured Bellows was right about not being able to head back east. "We'll have to dig in here," he said. "This looks to be the highest point of land around." The numbers were about even: seven or eight to six. But, counting the carbines on the cavalry mounts, they had eleven rifles, and that would give them an edge.

Running Wolf suddenly started jabbering something to Bellows. Slocum looked where he was pointing and saw a large force of cavalry moving through the trees beyond the creek, coming from the direction of the river.

"The colonel's not circling around," he said. "He's running. That's Troop G coming there."

The cavalry troop was moving at a trot. Likely the colonel had spotted them and turned tail before his own men were sighted, and the troop was just moving toward where they'd heard firing. That meant they'd probably heard the firing up here too.

He turned to Arthur. "What's to keep the colonel from joining up with Troop G? He could claim he ran onto me and Bellows holding you hostage. Join

Troop G and mount an attack to wipe us all out, you included. They can't afford to let you live now.''

''No chance of it,'' Arthur said. ''Most of them aren't even supposed to be in this territory. They'd have a hard time explaining why they're so far from their posts.''

Troop G had come to a halt down in the trees where the colonel's bunch had been. Slocum thought he saw a glint of light off a pair of field glasses pointing his way.

''They know we're up here,'' Bellows said. ''We got to do something. We can't hold off a whole cavalry troop.''

''What about it, Mr. President?'' Slocum said. ''We said we'd get you back to your people. There they are. Does that guarantee hold?''

Arthur still looked a little white in the face, but he had control of himself now. He watched the cavalry troop spreading out in a line along the far side of the creek, one man now clearly watching the bluff through a pair of field glasses. ''All right,'' he said. ''I made you a promise. I'll hold to it. You ought to be tried in a court of law, but you saved my life the other day, and you've foiled those who wanted to use my office for their own ends, so maybe it balances out. You put me on a horse and send me down there and I'll pull Troop G off your backs. We'll want them going after those others, anyway.''

''They're splitting up down there,'' Bellows said. ''Sending a detail to follow the tracks of the colonel's bunch. But I don't like the looks of that line the others are shaping up in.''

''Bring up one of those horses,'' Slocum said.

"We're going to send the President down there by himself."

Bellows looked at him. "You think that's smart? We ain't got a lot of running room."

"Mr. Arthur's said there'll be no pursuit and no prosecution. We'll take him at his word. I can't see that we have much choice, anyway."

Bellows obviously didn't like the idea, but if he had a better one in mind, he didn't come up with it. While he went to bring up one of the cavalry mounts, Slocum dug a white handkerchief out of his bag and tied it to the end of a little limb he'd cut off a nearby tree. He didn't want those troopers down there shooting Arthur before they realized who he was.

When Arthur was ready, Slocum led the horse down over the edge of the bluff into those trees masking the head of that little ravine they'd come up earlier.

Arthur mounted up and Slocum handed him the little white flag. "I'm not sure I can say it's been a pleasure knowing you, Mr. Slocum," Arthur said. "One thing I'll ask of you. Never say a word about this whole business to anybody. The country can't be allowed to know how close the government came to being brought down. If you hear anything at all, it will be that I wandered away from camp early this morning and got lost, and Troop G had to come find me. Anything else will be denied. That is how things work, you see."

"What about that log those lieutenant-colonels are keeping?"

Arthur smiled. "I'm afraid your good deed will have to be written out of it. By the time we get back to Washington, that log will be as insignificant as a young girl's diary. I'd suggest you and your friend take a long journey somewhere immediately. Somewhere very far away. And now I believe I will continue my vacation. I did promise Senator Vest I'd go take a look at his park. Goodbye, Mr. Slocum." He nudged the horse in the ribs and started down the ravine.

Slocum climbed back up over the rim of the bluff and joined Bellows and the scouts. Bellows was watching the ravine, where Arthur had just emerged from the trees.

"I can't say I like this," he said. "Ain't nothing stopping him from sending that bunch up here after us. Good as Running Wolf and his boys are, we'd never get away from that many troopers."

"We got no choice but to trust him," Slocum said. "We'll know as soon as he reaches them. Then they either go after the colonel or they come up here after us."

Arthur's mount was slowly making its way down the treeless hillside, the white handkerchief bobbing and dancing atop its pole. Now Slocum saw three cavalrymen splash across the creek and ride out to meet him—officers, but too far away to see just who. They met up with Arthur about halfway down the slope, snapping out a salute. Slocum watched one of them pointing up toward the bluff, then back to the creek, and Arthur doing some pointing now too, holding a little powwow. After a minute or two, the officers turned their mounts and escorted Arthur down the slope and into the trees across the creek.

"Don't mean nothing," Bellows said. "Not yet,

anyway. Could be they're just passing word on how many we are and how we're situated.''

Slocum watched one of the officers riding along the line, passing word on something, all right. Then the troopers began to pull out of the line, their horses milling around in the trees as they formed up in a column of twos, facing west. The officer waved them forward, and the whole column set off at a canter, heading up along the creek.

Bellows took off his hat and wiped a hand through his hair. "Well, I guess you were right. I guess we can breathe easy. I wasn't breathing at all there for a minute. Waiting's always worse than fighting. But what do you say we get the hell out of here, just the same? These boys can slip back onto the reservation without any trouble, but I don't figure this country's too healthy for us right now."

"I'll go along with that," Slocum said. "I'll feel a lot easier with a good long border between me and this country for a while."

19

Slocum woke at ten every morning to the pleasant sight of sunlight coming through the shutters of his room, the Mexican girl warm and brown and naked beside him, usually still asleep, sometimes murmuring something when she felt him come awake and reaching blindly out to pull him back so she could curl up in the hollow of his arms, her sleek black hair spilling across her bare shoulders. Usually he let her cuddle next to him for a few minutes more, until she was back in deep sleep. Then he would steal quietly out of the bed and put on his pants and send down for a pot of that good, strong Mexican coffee.

He would spend an hour on the balcony then, barefoot, drinking the coffee and smoking his first cigarette of the day, hearing chickens squawk in some yard a house or two away, watching the sun dappling the stones of the courtyard under the trees below the balcony and turning bright red the tiles of the roof across the way. When he had got his fill of that, he would go down the hall to roust Bellows out of bed, careful to knock first so as to give Bellows's girl time to put something on. Then they would all head out for a late breakfast in some cantina along a shady little side street.

Sometimes in the afternoons they would hire a rig

and take the girls for a drive out into the surrounding country, maybe finding a quiet stretch of riverbank for a swim, Bellows and Slocum lying lazily in the sun after one quick dip while the girls frolicked and splashed brown and naked and happy in the cool and rippling water. There were horse races to go to on Saturdays and some kind of festival in a village somewhere almost every week, and sometimes a religious procession would wake Slocum on a Sunday morning and he would go out to watch it from his balcony. But usually he got to bed too late to get up before ten; half the nights of the week were spent moving from one gambling dive to another, playing steadily and not winning very much, but enough to keep from dipping into what was left of the advance they'd got from the colonel.

This particular Thursday afternoon found them at a simple board table under a sunshade on a narrow sidewalk in the back part of town, Bellows smoking a cheroot with his after-breakfast coffee, Slocum trying with a pencil stub and a scrap of paper to total up his wins and losses from the night before. The girls had charmed them out of some cash for a spending spree and were off now somewhere buying more of that finery Mexican women seemed to like to wear: fancy black lace shawls, ivory combs, and dresses fitted so tight they made a man's breath hard to find. Slocum had sent for another pot of coffee, and this time when the waiter brought it out he had a newspaper with him.

"American paper," he said. "You want?"

Slocum hadn't given a thought to anything north of the border in a long while, but he accepted the paper, a Chicago *Sun,* close to two months old. He found the story right on the front page, under a good-sized headline.

"Look at this, Clay," he said, and showed him the headline.

PRESIDENT ARTHUR RETURNS
FROM WESTERN PACK-TRIP

Bellows blew a smoke ring and watched it drift up under the sunshade. "Let me know if my name's in the story. Otherwise I don't want to hear about it. I'm taking a siesta."

Slocum read the story through, but nothing in it surprised him. It was just as Arthur had said it would be.

"According to this, the President had a restful and interesting trip, the highlight of which was the trek through Yellowstone. Visited the Wind River reservation, where Chief Washakie of the Shoshone gave him a pinto pony for his daughter Nell. Caught a lot of trout. Killed three antelope, a bear, and a whole slew of game too small to itemize. That the way you remember it?"

"No," Bellows said. "No, it ain't. Not the highlight, anyway. I remember the highlight being a little different." He cocked an eye at Slocum. "How much you figure there is going on in this world people like you and me don't know about?"

"Quite a lot, I imagine."

"You know, nobody ever did convince me the colonel wasn't telling the truth. No matter what he wanted out of it. Could be Arthur was guilty as sin."

"I can't say I care much," Slocum said. "All I

care about I got right here. Something to bring in money. A pretty woman in my bed at night. A good breakfast, and good coffee and a cigarette after breakfast. What they do with the rest of the world is their business.''

He leafed through the pages of the newspaper, but there was nothing else of interest. He wondered how soon he would read other stories that told less than the whole story. Maybe a high-ranking general being quietly retired, or a politician quitting his post for reasons of ill health. He didn't care about that, either. He was out of it, and that was all he wanted.

EPILOGUE

Chester A. Arthur, twenty-first President of the United States, was elevated to that office not by election but by an assassin's bullet.

Representing the Stalwart faction of the Republican party—hostile to the South and upholding allegiance to Ulysses S. Grant—Arthur had run as the vice-presidential candidate on a ticket with James A. Garfield, whose GOP faction the Stalwarts derided as "Halfbreeds" because of their alleged lack of loyalty to the Republican cause. This attempt to unite the party foundered when, four months after their electoral victory, President Garfield was assassinated by Charles Guiteau.

Guiteau, a minor member of the Stalwart faction, had served during the campaign as a speechmaker and writer of political pamphlets in Arthur's home state of New York. After the election, an audience was arranged with Garfield, ostensibly so that Guiteau might request a diplomatic post. The request was denied. The assassination itself was carried out a short time later, and upon his apprehension, Guiteau blurted out that he was a Stalwart whose intent was to put his fellow Stalwart, Chester Arthur, in the White House.

After becoming President, Arthur personally pressed

for Guiteau's conviction, saying to Attorney General MacVeagh that he wanted "no slip." Guiteau stated at his trial that he had met with Arthur on more than one occasion and would "talk just as freely with him as I would with anybody," though claiming that no GOP leader had accepted his offer of help to the party. He described his assassination of President Garfield as "a political necessity." He was hanged on June 30, 1882, shouting from the gallows, "I saved my party and my land. Glory Hallelujah!" No suspicion of any involvement by Arthur in the assassination was ever made public.

Arthur was himself an ill man, however, learning in that same year that he was a victim of Bright's disease, a fatal kidney ailment. When the press noted his lack of vigor at the dedication of the Brooklyn Bridge in May of 1883, it was decided that the President needed a vacation, and arrangements were made for a pack-trip into Jackson Hole and Yellowstone Park.

President Arthur arrived by train in Green River, Wyoming Territory, in early August, accompanied by Secretary of War Robert Lincoln, General Philip Sheridan, Lieutenant-Colonel Michael Sheridan, the general's nephew, Lieutenant-Colonel James Gregory, Senator George Vest of Missouri, and other notables. After a stop at Fort Washakie in the Wind River reservation, where Chiefs Coal Black of the Arapaho and Washakie of the Shoshone conducted, for the Great White Father's entertainment, a sham battle with the seventy-five troopers of the expedition's escort—Troop G of the Fifth Cavalry—Arthur's party, a pack train of 175 packhorses and mules, departed on August ninth for a journey up into the Wind River range, across the continental divide, and down along the Gros Ventre River into Jackson Hole. A total press blackout had been imposed on the trip, General Sheridan himself threatening summarily to jail two Chicago reporters who attempted to attach themselves to the expedition. Once the party left Fort Washakie, there descended what one historian has called "a curtain . . . through which it is now impossible to see."

Over the years, various rumors about the President's pack-trip have reached public print. By some accounts, those present went on something of a spree. It is known that a band of Indians in Jackson Hole staged a war dance in honor of the Great White Father, and rumor persists that Arthur's life was saved from a possibly intoxicated brave brandishing a tomahawk only by the timely intervention of an unnamed member of his party. Among other published rumors is an account of a mysterious night-time incident during which a number of drunks in the encampment's "bar tent" killed several mules in a gun battle triggered by what they believed to be a raid by hostile Indians. Otherwise, we have only the official journal kept by Lieutenant-Colonels Gregory and Sheridan, whom one authority has accused of being "oblivious of their rare opportunity to report what may have been the most unusual vacation ever taken by any American President while still in office," and who describes their journal as "a prosaic travelogue . . . devoted almost exclusively to descriptions of the scenery and the number of fish caught."

According to later newspaper accounts, the President had an uneventful vacation and boarded a Northern Pacific train at Cinnabar, Montana on September 1, 1883, for the trip back to Washington. Arthur died three years later.

GREAT WESTERN YARNS FROM ONE OF THE BEST-SELLING WRITERS IN THE FIELD TODAY

JAKE LOGAN

JAKE LOGAN

_____	0-867-21217	SLOCUM AND THE MAD MAJOR	$1.95
_____	0-867-21120	SLOCUM AND THE WIDOW KATE	$1.95
_____	0-867-16880	SLOCUM'S BLOOD	$1.95
_____	0-867-16823	SLOCUM'S CODE	$1.95
_____	0-867-21071	SLOCUM'S DEBT	$1.95
_____	0-867-16867	SLOCUM'S FIRE	$1.95
_____	0-867-16856	SLOCUM'S FLAG	$1.95
_____	0-867-21015	SLOCUM'S GAMBLE	$1.95
_____	0-867-21090	SLOCUM'S GOLD	$1.95
_____	0-867-16841	SLOCUM'S GRAVE	$1.95
_____	0-867-21023	SLOCUM'S HELL	$1.95
_____	0-867-16764	SLOCUM'S RAGE	$1.95
_____	0-867-21087	SLOCUM'S REVENGE	$1.95
_____	0-867-16927	SLOCUM'S RUN	$1.95
_____	0-867-16936	SLOCUM'S SLAUGHTER	$1.95
_____	0-867-21163	SLOCUM'S WOMAN	$1.95
_____	0-867-16864	WHITE HELL	$1.95

All titles above carry Playboy ISBN prefix 0–867

Available at your local bookstore or return this form to:

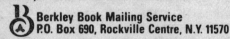

Berkley Book Mailing Service
P.O. Box 690, Rockville Centre, N.Y. 11570

Please send me the titles checked above. I enclose _____.
Include 75¢ for postage and handling if one book is ordered; 50¢ per book for
two to five. If six or more are ordered, postage is free. California, Illinois, New
York and Tennessee residents please add sales tax.

NAME _____

ADDRESS _____

CITY_____ STATE ZIP_____

Allow six weeks for delivery.